AF264822

Thanks to God for supporting me through the writing process. Thanks to my wife for her encouragement and writing some of the content, and thanks to our children who put up with their daddy disappearing to stare at the computer for long periods of time. Thanks to you for reading. I hope the journey means something to you.

DON'T MAKE ME STAY

David Willison

Seventh Exception Publishing House

Don't Make Me Stay

David Willison

Published by:
Seventh Exception Publishing House
Sydney Australia

Typesetting: David Willison

Cover Design: David Willison

ISBN: 978-0-646-85572-1

Dedicated to

all those who live,

or have lived

in out-of-home care.

Contents

CHAPTER I

Agency

It's limited

Dance music comes from a portable speaker. Skate shoes rock a skateboard back and forth above a large drop. Two teenage boys look up and watch, as a confident and determined teenage girl flies down the curve, over a hump, spins in the air, turns ninety degrees to the ground, twists and crashes down. Aleesha lets out a yelp of pain, but quickly pulls it back in. Kim rushes towards her.

'I'm fine. It's nothing,' Aleesha reassures Kim. She alternates between laughing and groaning as she pulls herself from the ground.

Kim returns to Charlie who has been filming her on his phone. His smile shows that he is still relishing the pain that she has on board. Aleesha goes back up to reset. She leans forward in pain, and pauses so that she can catch her breath.

A Police car drives into the parking lot behind her. Aleesha looks over her shoulder, and on seeing them yells, 'Po po!'

Aleesha runs flat out towards a fence on the opposite side of the park from the Police, throwing her skateboard over, and scaling the fence after it. The boys see the Police and peg it after her.

All three are breathing heavily as they climb the back fence of a large modern suburban house in a small Australian town. Charlie uses a bank card to open the side door and he goes in with the others following.

The next morning, Aleesha comes down the hallway to the dining room with epic bed hair. She throws a scrunched up drawing in the bin, then pauses next to a chart on the wall that has the residents' names. Aleesha moves closer to her column, and notices a red cross at the bottom.

'I wonder where I'll be sent next?' She says to Kim who is playing a video game in the open plan lounge room. Aleesha joins him on the couch and continues. 'I had this caseworker who let me change placement whenever I wanted.'

'Yeah?'

'Yeah, nah. It was great! I didn't have to wait for someone else to pull the plug. I could get the fuck out, when the shit was about to hit.... That's right. We had this thing where I'd do a countdown on the phone, "ten, nine...."'

Aleesha walks back to the chart.

'Matthew reckons I've burnt all my bridges now but.'

Aleesha walks towards the window and asks.

'You ever dream that you'll get a golden ticket to a place where you can sort the shit out in your head? Like without there being tonnes of people there, like... you know, shoveling more in?'

'Hey?'

'I'll take that as a 'no'.'

Kim glances at Aleesha and goes to say something, but doesn't.

'How can I get lots of money?' Aleesha wonders out loud.

'You live with Charlie, remember?!'

'Not like that.'

Matthew arrives at the front door, opens it, and leans in.

'Hello?' Matthew knocks on a closed door just inside the doorway because he isn't getting a response.

'We're doing hand over. Ten minutes' comes through the door in a tone that doesn't allow space for discussion.

'It's Matthew.'

The door opens quickly and Andrew smiles apologetically.

'Sorry! Thought you were one of them. Come on in.'

Andrew walks back to his chair in the office off the hallway with Loryn across the desk from him. He motions to Matthew to sit in an empty chair, and hands him some incident reports. Matthew scans through them and begins to look tired.

'What's the longest she can stay?'

'Sue only asked for a month, so that's all we quoted for.'

'I haven't been able to find anywhere else that'll take her,' Matthew complains.

'We might squeeze in an extra day for you. Unless she decides to, you know... not be her.' Neither Andrew or Matthew are looking confident about this last part.

Matthew takes a moment to compose himself, stands and walks to the door.

Matthew heads down the hallway to the lounge room and Kim pulls a face at Aleesha as Matthew walks in. Matthew notices this. Aleesha moves up the couch as Matthew sits.

'What are you doing to yourself?' he asks.

'Me?!' Aleesha tries to look surprised.

'Well the incident reports keep coming.'

'Umm. Don't believe everything you.... Have you even tried to find somewhere for me?'

Matthew looks away.

'Fuck. You have one job.'

'Aleesha...! We may have different views on what that is.'

'Clearly. You're reminding me that I need to take matters....'

'Aleesha. I wouldn't. You're only hurting yourself.'

'So you're going to help me?'

'I've told you. You're a teenager and I'm getting to the point where I can't do much for you. You keep making it harder for me. And you....'

'I'm not feeling sorry for you. You have one job. And you're own place to live.'

'About that. Sue and her manager want to give your bed here to someone else. I can't hold them off much longer.'

'Then get going. Quick, quick, quick!'

'Can't you... just, can't you just try to make it work here?'

'You're not even listening to me.' Matthew notices the increased intensity in her face.

'I don't know what that means but I'm thinking it's time I went.'

Matthew starts to leave and Aleesha throws her head back against the couch.

'Why don't you just leave her alone?' Kim asks he comes back into the room.

CHAPTER II

Wanted

Too many angles

Aleesha, Kim, and Charlie sneak out after dark. Kim and Charlie try car door handles to see if they're locked. At the third car, Charlie applies a coat hanger to a door and it pops opens. Charlie goes through the car, while Kim keeps a look out. He finds a lighter and a pocket knife. Kim joins in and finds an iPad under the seat. He avoids Charlie seeing it so that he can get it to Aleesha. Charlie starts to hide the things he found in nearby bushes.

When Kim gets to Aleesha she's on Facebook on her phone.

'Look what I got you!'

'No, no, no. Kim. No.'

'Sure?!'

'Yes. I don't want anything to do with that.' Kim runs the iPad over to Charlie who hides it under his hoodie.

Kim rejoins Aleesha.

'Shit,' Aleesha says.

'What?'

'Mum's profile came up on Facebook.'

'Did you message her?'

'Umm. Message her?!. Umm. She wouldn't reply anyway.'

'Why not?'

'Because she's a, um, a selfish, self-involved primordial cow who never gave a fuck about me?!'

'What? Um.... I haven't seen you go on family contact have I?'

'Haven't seen her for a couple of years.'

'Fuck!'

'Yeah. She's left more than her fair share up here.' Aleesha gestures at her head.

Charlie finishes hiding the objects and heads down the road with Kim and Aleesha following. Charlie turns back towards Aleesha and yells.

'You gonna show me how to do that trick?'

'Get someone else.'

'You better or you'll regret it.'

Kim turns to Aleesha.

'I've been asking you for ages!'

'Fuck Kim. I don't even... I need to keep Charlie... you know? But he's gonna get it when the time comes. Believe me.'

Kim sits on the edge of the skate bowl. Aleesha is showing Charlie how to do a trick on her skateboard.

Charlie tries the trick Aleesha showed him. He crashes, gets up and runs and shoves her to the ground.

'Fuck tonne of help you are. Look what you did to me.'

Aleesha slowly sits up and looks up at him. Charlie moves to stand over her more but pauses on seeing a Police car arrive in the car park.

'Let's go Aleesha' comes over the loud speaker from Officer Price. Aleesha looks at the fence.

'Not this time' Officer Price warns. Aleesha's posture drops. Aleesha glances at the police car. She heads towards it with Kim following, and they get in. Charlie shrugs and walks towards the car.

Officer Price watches Charlie approach, and gets out of the car.

'Back here' she directs.

Officer Price goes to open the back cell part of the paddy wagon.

'Why do I have to go in the back? Put her back here.'

Officer Price puts her hand on his shoulder and firmly directs him in.

They pull out of the car park with Aleesha and Kim in the backseats.

'You guys been up to anything?'

Aleesha looks worriedly at Kim.

'Yeah. Skating?'

'You haven't noticed anyone breaking into cars then?'

'I didn't touch no car,' Aleesha replies.

'I asked if you saw anyone....'

Aleesha is panicked and tries to focus on her breathing. Kim looks at the floor.

'I've got enough shit of my own, to go down for someone else's' Aleesha whispers to Kim.

'Hey?'

'I'm not going to stay standing still in wet concrete.'

'What?'

'I'm not waiting around for things to go to shit again.' Aleesha looks at Kim with annoyance then looks out the window, massaging her temples.

Aleesha and Kim head swiftly in when they get back to avoid being around for Officer Price to release Charlie. They know he's going to go for them when he gets the chance. They quickly go into Aleesha's room, shut the door and sit up against it as they hear the front door slam. After what seems like an endless gap in time – which is in fact very short, they both jolt forwards with the force that Charlie has applied to the door. After what Aleesha feels has been a sufficiently long period, she sneaks out to the toilet. As she returns she jumps out of her skin when she sees that Charlie is standing in his doorway watching her.

'You tried to get me in trouble with Price as well?!'

'Chill Charlie. Chill.'

'No where else will take you, hey?'

'What?'

'You're nothing. No one wants you and they don't even want you here.'

'Maybe I don't want to be wanted anyway Charlie.'

'You don't have a choice. You can't look after yourself can you?!' Charlie lets out a delighted snicker but then quietens as he hears movement in the staff room.

Aleesha takes the opportunity to make it back to her room and sit up against the door and rolls her eyes at Kim who is passed out on the floor. Thoughts rush back into her head which she has kept at a distance for some time. Does she have to rely on other people? Can she be independent? How would that look? She shakes her head to escape this mental deluge. There is some excitement to the idea of independence, but it also feels completely impossible. Or terrifying. She isn't sure which, and she doesn't want to find out.

CHAPTER III

Pumping

All or nothing

Aleesha is pacing in the lounge room in the morning when Loryn comes in.

'You've got another strike for absconding, and one for Charlie getting hurt on your skateboard. You're on your last legs.'

'What?!'

Charlie walks into the room. Their eyes meet.

'You're responsible for Charlie getting hurt. You're older than him so you should be making good decisions that keep him safe. I've told you a million times.'

'Yeah Aleesha. It's like you don't even care about me at all.' Charlie is enjoying his smirk.

Aleesha looks at Loryn who remains looking at her. Aleesha glances at Charlie, then turns back to Loryn.

'What the actual...?!'

Loryn walks out the side of the house which Aleesha watches. Aleesha heads over and rips her behaviour chart off the wall. She tries to scrunch it up to fit it in the bin. She has difficulty with this, places it over the bin, and stomps it in.

'Loryn!' Charlie yells out with glee.

Aleesha looks concerned but is then happy that at least she has completed her task. Charlie sits on the couch smiling to himself and Aleesha walks to the side door.

Aleesha approaches Loryn and her co-worker Erin who are drinking coffee as they lean against the wall. Erin and Loryn don't notice her approach.

'Now she's wanting to come with me on the three hour drive to pick up Gavin' Erin complains to Loryn.

'I'm sorry for Charlie getting hurt. I feel really bad about that…. Can you please take me into town this arvie?'

Loryn and Erin turn to look at Aleesha.

'You've lost free time for the next month remember?'

'Andrew said I could.'

'No he didn't. Don't try me. You need to make good choices.'

'Please? I really need to go into town.'

'Why?'

'To see a friend?'

'You don't have any.'

'Shut up Loryn. You don't know me.'

'You're a child Aleesha. You don't get to make all the decisions.'

Aleesha turns to Erin.

'Please Erin. Can you help me?'

Erin shakes her head, drinks from her coffee, and turns back to Loryn.

'I really don't want her to come with me. She treats me like a preschooler. She's an educator and that spills over I think.'

Aleesha walks back into the lounge room and sits on the couch beside Kim who is playing a video game.

'Why don't you do anything useful?'

'What?'

'You can do anything you want Kim.'

'Um. No I can't.'

Aleesha leans towards Kim quickly, causing him to shrink back, and she raises her voice with a playful smile.

'Yes you fucking can!'

Aleesha lowers her voice, 'Well I fuckin can. They're going take me into town one way or a-fuckin-nother.'

Aleesha walks quickly to the hallway towards her bedroom where she frustratedly picks up some of her clothes and throws them in a back pack that already has clothes in it. She pulls some drawings off the wall, puts them in a sketchbook, and into her bag. She picks up her bag and skateboard, hurries to the bedside table, and extracts a Stanley knife hidden behind the back of the draw.

Aleesha rushes past the lounge room, where Andrew and Kim watch her pass into the hallway. Andrew sees the knife and starts towards Aleesha. Kim's eyes widen.

Aleesha drops her things on the floor beside the bathroom door, enters, slams the door, and locks herself in.

Andrew yells towards the side door to get Loryn and Erin's attention.

'Code red. Bathroom.'

Andrew goes to the bathroom door.

'Aleesha? We don't want to see you hurt yourself. Remember to make good choices.'

'I'm not coming out unless you promise to take me into town. And I mean like now.'

Andrew starts to unlock the door from outside, but Aleesha locks it again. Erin joins Andrew in the hallway and makes a call.

'Police?'

Officer Price arrives and takes notes from Erin before walking down the side of the house to the door into the lounge room. Officer Price walks past Kim, who is looking pale and glancing around nervously. She approaches the bathroom door where Andrew is still trying to get the door open.

'Hey Andrew. I've got this.'

Andrew looks up, lets go of the door handle and moves out of the way. Kim peers down the hallway at them. Charlie is the other side of them near the front door recording with his phone.

'Fuck... that was deep' Aleesha says intensely.

Officer Price freezes, physically orients herself, and kicks the door open. Aleesha is standing next to the sink where the knife is in clear view.

'I can't go on' Aleesha advises as she raises her hands and clasps them behind her head.

Officer Price puts the knife in her pocket and gets her handcuffs out.

'You don't have to handcuff me. I'm suicidal not homicidal.'

Officer Price puts the handcuffs on Aleesha.

'And every time we get you assessed, so we can check that out. You know that.... Let's go."

Aleesha sighs and rolls her eyes. Officer Price pushes Aleesha out into the hallway.

Aleesha looks at her bag and skateboard.

'Could you be a love and get those for me? It always takes so long before I see anyone and I don't trust these scoundrels.'

Officer Price gives a nod to Andrew who picks up Aleesha's bag and skateboard as she escorts Aleesha down the hallway towards Charlie and the front door.

As they come closer to Charlie, Aleesha spins away from Officer Price and head-butts Charlie hard. Officer Price swiftly puts her leg in front of Aleesha, and crunches Aleesha into the floor. Aleesha lets out a gasp.

'I'm trying to help you. Work with me a little hey?'

'Fuuccckkk!' Aleesha gasps. 'Okay, okay, okay. Maybe I'm a little homicidal as well. But don't tell the nurse?!"

Officer Price stands Aleesha up. Aleesha makes eye contact with Charlie who is putting a lot of pressure on his nose, and holding back the tears which are glistening.

"If I see you again...." Charlie says as he tries to appear convincing.

Aleesha smiles then lets her smile drop which startles Charlie.

Officer Price opens the door to the police car. Aleesha turns to look at Kim who has followed her out, and stopped just outside the front door.

"Ten, nine..." Aleesha counts down.

Kim has tears in his eyes. Aleesha gets in the car and Officer Price puts her bag and skateboard on the seat beside her.

The Police car climbs the mountain range on the way into Toowoomba, Queensland's largest inland city, not long after the sun has set. Aleesha leans her head against the car window and looks up at the street lights as she passes under them.

They arrive at the ambulance entry of Toowoomba Base Hospital where Aleesha is shown to a secure room.

Officer Price leaves as a large and serious looking security guard takes over from the nurse. The security guard stands in the doorway as Aleesha tries to cope with the cool temperature of the bolted down bench which is the only piece of furniture in the room. Aleesha slowly tries to rub some warmth into her body.

She pulls her sketchbook out of her bag and continues a drawing. The drawing is of a cartoon girl with wings that she is trying to stretch out but is having trouble due to the obstacles around her.

Aleesha feels some satisfaction with the drawing but then all the thoughts that she spends a lot of time keeping out, start to come back in.

She attempts to disrupt the thought flow by scrolling through Facebook, looking for a different feeling to replace her current one. She does a double take at a picture of her mother in a hospital bed that says, 'back in Toowoomba Base Hospital.' Aleesha freezes. Puts her phone down. Picks it up and checks it again and barely acknowledges the nurse who has come back to ask more questions. The nurse gives up and leaves as Aleesha doesn't appear home.

'You couldn't just let me out for a liiittle walk… for some fresh air, could you?' Aleesha asks the security guard when her attention comes back to the present.

'No.'

'But my mental health is just dandy, like I already told the nurse.'

The security guard doesn't want to get drawn into conversation and is thankful to be able to look down the hallway at a disheveled drunk man shouting at a nurse and in general. A slim female nurse then pushes him down into the bed and adjusts her weight to generate more downward force.

Aleesha pokes her head around the corner and the security guard moves to block her from exiting.

'It looks like she could use some help. I think he's about to work his right arm free. You see it?'

'No?'

The security guard steps backwards and moves from side to side in the hallway to try to get a better view of the man's right arm which is out of view.

As she is doing this, Aleesha comes flying out of the doorway with her skateboard and bag and slams into the security guard who staggers and falls backwards against the wall.

'Sorry!'

Aleesha starts to run up the corridor to the exit and the security guard launches herself towards Aleesha. Aleesha pumps her legs to keep moving forwards.

The drunk man looks at the commotion, and lets out a cheer as Aleesha flies out the exit.

'Yeah girlie. That's what I'm talking bout!'

The nurse pushes him back down on the bed.

CHAPTER IV

Meeting

Denial

Aleesha runs to a hedge. The security guard comes out and looks around. She is holding her side and decides to call this a loss and move on so she returns inside.

After waiting for what she feels like is enough time for the security guard to find something else meaningful to do, Aleesha walks in the front door of the hospital. She picks a corridor to walk up. Aleesha sees another security guard and she freezes. She sees him stop to talk to a nurse, so she sucks in a breath and walks past him. She explores what feels like a maze of corridors and dead ends, peering into rooms that she can see into when this is possible, while trying not to draw too much attention to herself.

Aleesha reaches the end of a corridor as it starts to get light and looks tentatively around the corner. She moves past a nurses station and looks into a single room where she sees into a woman in her thirties who looks older than she should. Aleesha tries to get a better look. She looks back towards the nurses station and a nurse looks up at her so she darts into the room.

Aleesha moves closer to the woman in the bed whose eyes are closed. Aleesha freezes and then brings herself to the present and turns and starts to leave.

'Aleesha?' the woman asks.

'No.'

Aleesha stops. Turns back.

'What... why... what are you doing here?' the woman asks.

'I'm not.'

Aleesha rubs her face with both hands, and massages her temples.

'Well?' the woman persists.

'What?'

'Are you right in the head?'

'Yeah?'

'You're obviously lost. So why don't you take a tiny moment, and then retrace your steps?'

Aleesha stares at her mother.

'What are you looking at?' Rachel asks.

Aleesha looks away and Rachel keeps the pressure on.

'Well?'

'I don't know. I just saw... you on Facebook, that you were here too....'

'I'd help show you the way out... but....'

Rachel looks down at her emaciated body. Aleesha stares at Rachel, and rubs her head again.

'Are you high?'

Aleesha slowly shakes her head. Rachel realises something so she reaches out and gingerly puts a photo frame of her and a man face down. Aleesha looks up, walks towards Rachel, and rights the picture frame which Rachel is too slow to stop.

'Is that... Uncle Quade?'

Rachel nods as she is out of ideas how else to respond.

'Still looks nothing like dad.... Matthew told me dad died.'

'Don't talk about him or I'll....'

Aleesha picks at some dust on her clothes.

'Is it bad?'

Rachel nods her head minimally. Aleesha pulls a chair from near the door to be beside Rachel's bed. Rachel breaks eye contact.

'How bad?'

'I may last a month, if I don't get upset or eat anything nice.'

Aleesha looks at her shoes as some moisture gathers in her eyes.

'Stop that' Rachel barks in a crusty dry sound.

Aleesha straightens.

'I have to pee.'

Rachel starts to smile and then stifles it as Aleesha speeds out.

Aleesha rushes up on the desk.

'Which one of you is looking after Rachel Brown?'

Doctor Wilcox returns eye contact.

'That would be me.'

Aleesha raises her voice.

'Well what are you doing? Why are you just sitting there?'

The doctor stands up and walks around to her.

'Let's go and talk in there.'

He nods towards a meeting room, and ushers her towards it. She walks ahead of him, glancing back at him as she goes. Once in, he closes the door behind him and Aleesha looks around him at the door, uncertain, and then steels herself.

'So what are you doing to help my mum?'

'And who might you be?'

'Her daughter? Aleesha... Brown.'

'I haven't seen anything in the notes....'

'Aw come on. Get on with it. I look just like her dumbass. And how often does someone come in at 5 in the morning and pretend to be someone's daughter?'

'Okay. Well. Let's start with what she has shall we? She has chronic ischaemic heart disease.'

Aleesha stares at him.

'Not enough blood and oxygen are getting to her heart, and she's had two heart attacks already. Each one that she has, increases the chances that she will have another one, and that that one will kill her.'

'Great. So what are you doing about it?'

'Just a tip that you might want to remember... is that I don't work for you. And, if you want to get things from people, you may not want to push them as hard.'

'Thanks for the tip wise one. Am I, like scaring you?!'

'You're making me uncomfortable, yes.'

'Sorry doctor. Sir.'

Aleesha whispers and speaks softly, almost to a whisper.

'Can you please let me know how you're helping my mum to get better, so that she can come home and look after me?'

Doctor Wilcox looks confused and pauses.

'I didn't know she.... So, she needs to stop eating what she was, and, we may be able to make a hole in her heart with a laser, so that the blood flows out better. We can't do anything else, because her heart tissue is too stiff.'

'She's hard hearted? I wish someone had told me sooner.'

Doctor Wilcox regards her suspiciously.

'Stiff. Well the tissue anyway.'

'Okay. So that all sounds very complicated, and it sounds like you, well... know what you're doing, soooo....'

'Remember to ease up on bailing people up for me, okay?'

'Sure, sure. Thanks. What are you doing later?'

'What?'

'It's looking like I'm need somewhere to sta.... Nothing.

Doctor Wilcox leaves, and Aleesha follows him out.

Aleesha comes back through the door to her mother while busily scrolling on her phone.

'Just checking that they know what they're doing. Ischeamic….'

'Who are you here with?'

'Ummm. My fan club. My army of one?'

'Now that you know why I'm here. Why are you?'

'Done now. I got myself brought in for a mental health review.'

'What? Who does that?'

'Me apparently.'

'How'd you fare?! I'm surprised they let you out.'

'They didn't. I didn't ask permission.'

Rachel laughs.

'You really shouldn't have come here.'

'You shouldn't be dying, so let's say we're even.'

'Whatever. You gonna call them to come and get you?'

'Nah. I've left those fuckers behind. I think….'

'Really? What the fuck makes you think I'm going to look after you?'

'Mum, come on, you haven't done that for a while now. But I'm here to help, well, you!'

'Shut up Leesh. That's not my fault… Ahh, I can't do this anymore. Get out.'

Aleesha turns to leave, then turns back. Rachel's face remains hardened. Aleesha leaves. Rachel sinks back in her bed and closes her eyes.

Aleesha comes back through the door.

'I was just kidding, I'm not done!'

'Shit. You're killing me.'

'Nup. That's a whole cup of not my fault.'

Rachel looks at her blankly. Aleesha sits down, and Rachel looks at the wall in front of her.

'Any ideas on where I can stay?'

'Why the fuck would that concern me?'

'But like. You could try to help a little?'

Rachel glares at Aleesha, who looks away, then looks back again.

'I'm not going back.'

'Why would you? They feed you and put a roof over you, you ungrateful little brat.'

'Yeah.... I wasn't asking for your permission.'

'If you have all the answers....'

'I've got to find somewhere, like, Uncle Quade's?'

'No.'

'Why not?'

'Because I said.... You're still a baby, and you need to go the fuck back to where you came from.'

Aleesha gets tears, then hardens.

'So it's on me. A-fucken-gain. To find someone more useful than you... a-gain.'

'Why the fuck are you still here running your mouth? Fuck off and sort shit out for yourself kid rock.'

Aleesha looks at the door, at her mother, at the door again. She turns back to her mother. Rachel tilts her head to the door.

Aleesha looks at it, and then swipes the bread roll from Rachel's table and runs out.

Aleesha comes out of the hospital doors and is daunted by how bright it is. She rings Kim.

'This isn't going well…! I'm not throwing in the towel that easy, because I can make it on my own. You'll fuckin see…. No. You're the one being fucking stupid. At least I'm fucking trying something…. Ahh, get fucked Kim.'

Aleesha hangs up. A young man in his twenties approaches. Aleesha runs her hands through her hair, and twirls it while smiling at him. He doesn't notice her. Aleesha deflates.

CHAPTER V

Contrast

Can soothe

Aleesha rides up to a public bench which is near a restaurant where people are sitting outside. Aleesha sits and gets out a sketch book and starts a drawing of a skater girl who is trying to cast a spell.

Aleesha looks over at a tall young man in his late teens with his back to her, sitting across from his parents.

'The perfect girl for you probably lives somewhere else!' his mother says.

'I wouldn't spend too much time worrying about her, son. She means well but she seems to rub people the wrong way anyway' his dad adds.

'It'll probably sort itself out' Ben suggests.

'I'm so blessed to have you as my son. You're growing into the most beautiful man.'

Aleesha looks away as Sally leans over the table and kisses Ben on the cheek and the forehead. Sally sits back and Bradley hugs Ben across the table.

'Love you Ben'

'Love you dad.'

Aleesha gags a little, coughs and shakes her head. Ben turns to look towards the sound, and Aleesha quickly resumes drawing. Aleesha continues the drawing, and it's near completion.

Aleesha looks back to where Ben was, and sees him out the front of the tables, hugging his parents goodbye. Aleesha runs her hands through her hair, and smooths her clothes.

Ben's parents leave in the opposite direction to her, and Ben goes to go past her whilst writing on his phone. Ben starts to look towards Aleesha, and she puts on her best smile, but he doesn't notice and keeps walking. Aleesha's shoulders drop.

Once past her, Ben stops short of bumping into a light pole, sees a message light up on his phone, turns to look after his parents, and runs back towards them. Aleesha waves at him, but he doesn't see. As he is about to pass her, she rolls her skateboard forward, causing him to trip and fall over.

Aleesha jumps with surprise at his crash. Ben looks up from the sidewalk at Aleesha and she smiles sweetly.

'I felt that' she adds with concern.

'Sorry. Is your board okay?'

'Yeah, yeah, yeah. How about you?!'

Ben stands and takes a look at Aleesha's drawing which she pulls closer to herself.

'You're very talented.'

'I'm not drawing for attention or like busking or anything....'

Ben smiles and sits beside her.

'I'm Ben.'

Ben offers his hand. Aleesha looks at his hand and withdraws up the bench. Smiling, he returns his hand to his lap, and starts rubbing his knees before turning back to her.

'Are you from round here?'

'Um... Gold Coast.'

'Really? Cool.'

Ben looks at the drawing.

'Who is that?'

'No one. Me. I dunno.... It just looks cute to me.'

'I think it's great. I wish I was able to be artistic.'

'What are you then?'

'What do you mean?'

'If you're not artistic, you must be something else?'

'That's a good question! I dunno what I am.'

'Well there's a puzzle for you to work on.'

'Thanks. Though I wish someone else was the main character.'

'You're not for introspection then?!'

'Intro what? I don't even know what that is.'

'Then you clearly haven't had shii.... Um....'

'Science. Facts and figures and the like.'

'What?'

'I guess I'm the scientific guy.'

'Ewww.... Umm.... I haven't met one of those for a while. I could use more facts and figures in my life I spose.'

'Really?'

'Not really. I could probably just Google what I need.'

They both laugh. Aleesha puts her sketch book back in her back pack.

'Do you know Will Eisner?'

'You don't!'

'Yeah I do.'

'That's so weird.'

'Errrm. My favourite one of his is Sheena, Queen of the Jungle, holding The Spirit, and Uncle Sam and the Hawks of the Sea are on the other side. There's a boat in the middle in a one-point perspective, which makes it feel like the characters are bursting out of the page.

'Yeah. I know it. Sheena was the first female comic...'

'...book character with her own title.' Ben completes.

'I've gotta say I'm impressed. Well, it was great meeting you.' Aleesha gets her backpack and skateboard.

'Are you off?'

Ben stands as Aleesha stands.

'What are you doing tomorrow?' Aleesha asks with warm smile.

'Um... church.'

'Great. You're one of....'

'Okay... wait, did you wanna come? I'm not sure you'd like it though....'

'If you were asking me to do, well, basically anything else, I would... I mean, wait, I take that back... I might, and I mean I might want to?!'

Ben smiles.

'You know what? You should come. I could introduce you to my friends seeing as you're new in town, and we'll have something to eat at some point after.

Aleesha looks at her tummy.

'Ummm. Ummm... okay?'

'Ahhh, really?'

'Yeah. Okay then.'

'Ermm.... Okay. It's that triangle church just up from the skate park on James and North. I'll see you there at 11?'

Aleesha walks out the back of the hospital and sits on the lawn sloping down a hill where no one can see her.

She draws a cartoon girl in bed looking out from under the covers. She finishes, lies back, and rolls on her side. Thoughts rush in about how to move forward with these thoughts being interspersed with present considerations like wondering why grass makes you feel itchy.

Aleesha tosses and turns and manages to fall asleep. She wakes up with a start and looks around to remind herself of where she is and who she is. Reality comes back with a vengeance and she's particularly annoyed that her sleep hasn't carried her through to the morning.

She lies back and adjusts her position to try to get more comfortable and adjusts her clothes to try to maintain some warmth. Aleesha squirms and then hits the ground with her fist, stands and walks towards the hospital.

Aleesha walks in the emergency exit and heads to the toilets happy that no one seems to be alert to anything happening in the waiting room. Once in the toilet, she splashes her face with water and looks at herself in the mirror. She appears to lose focus but then brings her focus back and splashes her face again.

Aleesha leaves the hospital and approaches where she was lying. She lies down on her back looking up at the sky. She adjusts her body to try to get comfortable and then falls asleep.

Aleesha wakes and changes her clothes in the hospital toilet before going to the hospital car park, and kicks off on her skateboard.

She passes the church so that she know where to be at 11 and comes to a skate park. Aleesha does a circuit of the skate park, pulling off her first few tricks but ends up going flying on a trick that she's still trying to master.

She approaches the guys on skateboards but they won't acknowledge her. She is pained by being ignored and stops and sits where she can watch what is going on.

Two parents are helping a 3 year old girl to ride a balance bike and Aleesha smiles while watching them. Aleesha stands, sniffs her underarms, straightens her hair, and then kicks off down the road.

When she sees Ben waiting for her, she hops off her skateboard and carries it as she approaches him. She looks at a reflection of herself in a window and self-consciously smooths her hair.

'You okay?' Ben greets her.

'Um... mum's dying, and I'm at a church. Maybe I should go in and light a candle or something.'

'That sucks. About your mum I mean. Um. We don't have any candles. Uh. Yeah.'

Ben and Aleesha walk side by side into the church at first but Ben gets slightly ahead to get past some people. He sits in a pew beside Simon, Nick and Emma. Aleesha goes towards the gap beside him next to the aisle, but Sophie who has been talking to a couple in the adjacent row of pews, speeds up to get there first.

Sophie sits down and looks up at Aleesha who has stopped, clenching her fists. Sophie looks her up and down with a look of annoyance. Aleesha looks at Ben. He smiles at her but doesn't offer a way forwards so Aleesha sits down in the pew behind. Sophie sees Ben give Aleesha another smile.

'Who's that?' Sophie asks.

'Aleesha.'

Sophie looks back at Aleesha.

'She didn't have to wear a dress, but she could've at least brushed her hair. And who brings a skateboard into a church?'

Aleesha stays staring ahead and starts to reach for her hair but stops herself. Ben lowers his voice.

'She can hear you.'

Sophie smiles and shrugs her shoulders.

An elder stands up. Aleesha stands and slides out of the pew as he starts to do the welcome and walks towards the back.

'I'd like to welcome all the visitors that we have today. And our members. It's great to worship together with the saints,'

Aleesha finds a toilet is looking at herself in the mirror. She runs her hands through her hair. She moves forward and checks her face and then her teeth. Aleesha stands back and runs her hands over any crumples in her shirt. She goes to run her hands over her jeans but stops and puts her hands on top of her head and lets out a breath. She drops her hands, straightens her hair again and heads for the door.

Aleesha returns to her seat. Ben glances back at Aleesha with a smile. Aleesha notices but screws up her face a little back at him. He turns back to face the front.

Pastor Arnold walks onto the stage.

'Recently I was taken aback by, there's a..., there's something that went crazy on social media. There was an old man in Wollongong, who had recently lost his golf partner. His wife had died many years prior, and being a modern man, he advertised online for a golf partner, for someone facing a similar situation. Apparently he had offers from all over the country, and people basically offering to fly him to different golf courses all over the place, just for one game. So it made me wonder whether we as a church could tap into this in some way. Whether we could have some sort of social media outlet, um, or service, something along the lines of a site that advertises things for sale, that runs along the idea of "adopt-a-buddy." We as church could help people connect with each other, and show our heart for service as well.'

Charlotte who is standing up the back, shakes her head, audibly sighs and quietly mutters.

'Like we wouldn't screw that up too.' She checks to see if anyone is looking at her but no one is so she reassures herself that she hasn't been heard to be more mindful next time she has an opinion in church.

In the process of everyone one filling out Ben ends up sitting with the others on couches near the entrance. Aleesha passes to leave and Ben jumps up. Sophie watches.

'How'd you go?'

Aleesha mimics sitting and standing and being unsure which to do next by jerking around a bit.

'It makes sense eventually. Do you want to get some food?'

Sophie speeds to Ben's side and takes his arm.

'We're going to the park again like we always do.'

Sophie pulls on Ben's arm.

'Park?... Why?' Aleesha asks.

'Uh. I dunno. It's what we do I guess.' Ben replies.

Tiana who is 6 years of age, rides her skateboard past Aleesha, Ben, Simon, Nick, Sophie and Emma who are sitting in a circle in the park next to the skate park. Tiana gingerly does a circuit of the skate park, hits an uneven part and falls flat on her face.

Aleesha stands and has a pained look as she starts to walk towards Tiana, but Sophie and Emma who have noticed Aleesha watching Tiana are ahead and get there before her. Aleesha stops but is close.

'You totally deserved that. What are you doing?' Sophie demands.

'Uh....' Tiana is taken aback.

'You know what day it is don't you?'

'Yeah?'

'Does your mum know you're here? Emma chimes in.

'Yeah.'

'Really?' Sophie asks.

'Yes.'

Sophie and Emma are standing over Tiana.

'You're even still in your church clothes. Get out of here, now. You're embarrassing us,' Sophie directs.

'And yourself,' Emma adds.

Tiana gets tears in her eyes, gets up, picks up her skateboard, and limps away. Sophie and Emma turn and walk towards where they were. Aleesha looks stunned and doesn't know where to look but Sophie and Emma don't pay attention to her.

Ben walks towards Aleesha.

'What the heck was that about? I'm not so sure those two are making good choices.'

'We're not meant to play today. It's like the seventh day is different to the other six.. For resting... Um.... It's complicated, don't worry about it.'

'I think she's worried about it.' Aleesha gestures at Tiana.

'Don't worry about the girls. They've got good hearts.'

'Right. That's completely not what it looks like.'

Aleesha goes to catch up with Tiana but she sees Charlotte approach Tiana and give her a long hug. Aleesha turns back to Ben.

'I'm off to see mum.'

'Do you want to um... uh... meet us later? It's a pity you're going to miss lunch, but can you come to Soph's, say around 5:30?'

'Ummmm.'

'It's a BBQ.'

Aleesha rubs her belly.

'Um. We'll see. Put your number in my phone.'

Aleesha pretends to continue to use her phone while Ben, Simon, Nick, Sophie and Emma leave before heading over to where Charlotte and Tiana sitting.

'What was those guys problem?'

'Hey?' Charlotte looks up.

'Sophie and Emma were giving her curry.'

'Uhhh. They're…. Um. A bit, well. It's hard to explain.'

'You alright though?' Aleesha asks Tiana.

'Yep.'

'Cool. Cool. Just checking.'

Aleesha leaves and Charlotte watches her.

CHAPTER VI

Red man

Can he be trusted?

Aleesha walks gingerly towards Rachel's bed. Rachel sags on seeing her.

'Awww, no. What the actual fuck?'

'How are ya?'

'Being stuck in bed gets even worse every time you walk in.'

Aleesha looks deflated and looks at the floor.

'Fuck me mum. You really are a dry black cloud aren't you?'

'Fuck. I haven't heard that for ages. Your dad used to say that.'

'I remember.'

'Well... what do you want?'

'I dunno.'

Aleesha pulls up a chair.

'I met a boy.'

'Well fuck me, I'm impressed. Because there aren't gonna be many of those after your naive little arse.'

'Ben.'

'Uh huh. Where is he?'

'I'm gonna see him after this.'

'Has he taken you in, has he?'

'BBQ at his friend's house. And he's Christian which means he has to help me.'

'Really? And how has he helped you miss training bra?'

'Have you thought about me staying with Uncle Quade for a bit? While I get things going with Ben and his friends that is?'

'Don't ask that again.'

A message alert goes off on Aleesha's phone and she pulls it out of her pocket.

'Sorry.'

Aleesha puts her phone on silent and reads the message, 'Meet you at the North Street bus stop in 5?'

Aleesha texts back, 'Sure.'

Aleesha turns back to her mum.

'So, what have you been up to? Anything important?'

Rachel stiffens and tries to choose an answer.

'This and that.'

'But like. What have you been doing?'

'What the fuck are you asking baby driver?'

'Um....'

Aleesha turns to leave.

'Use protection!'

Aleesha looks confused and keeps going.

Aleesha comes around the corner of a corridor in the hospital and Matthew watches this. Aleesha sees him and jumps with fright.

'Shit Matthew.... You shouldn't creep up on people like that.'

'Are you out of your mind?'

Aleesha looks shocked.

'I told you not to get kicked out, and you left?'

'They were about to. Don't tell me they weren't.'

'You don't miss a beat do you? I shouldn't even be here. You're a teenager, and, Sue said....'

'Yes?'

'You're too... old and the younger kids are the priority. Especially as you're self-placing instead of doing what you should.'

'So you wouldn't have anywhere for me, even I found a way to not be radioactive?'

'Ummm.'

'Ah well. Thanks for your help.'

Aleesha leaves and Matthew looks undecided about what to do next.

Aleesha rides up to Ben and she picks up her skateboard. Ben stands from the bus stop bench and starts walking with Aleesha joining him as it starts to get dark.

'Do you miss the coast?'

'What?'

'The Gold Coast?'

'Oh right. Nup. Not really. I was stuck with some real, not headed anywhere good typos. Too much has happened to them and it's stuck to them.'

'What?'

Residential care. Foster care. Not with the mummys and the daddys.

'Oh. That sounds intense.'

Aleesha looks thoughtful.

'I am.'

Aleesha laughs.

'I mean it is, yes, yes. I'm not intense. I'm chilled!'

'You look like a coast chick.'

Aleesha smiles big.

'Thanks!'

'So you're still in care? You said something about your mum.'

'Sort of. They keep not coping with me and kicking me out, so now there's no where that'll take me, leaving me up shiii....'

Ben stops at a intersection and Aleesha continues to cross. Aleesha looks back and sees that Ben is back at the light, and she stops in the middle of the road.

'What are you doing?'

'There's a red man. It means wait. It's not safe to cross.'

'Ignore the red man. He's not real, and he won't mind.'

Ben cautiously shakes his head.

'Aww come on. I'm hungry. The red man doesn't have a brain. I do, and I say you're good to go. So let's go.'

Ben shakes his head even though there are no cars around.

'6,227 pedestrians died crossing the road last year.'

Aleesha starts walking back to Ben with a dramatic sigh.

'Why is it a man anyway? Are men more authoritative or something? But if it was Sheena, you'd be standing there even longer watching her in slow motion I'm sure. Fine fine. I'll wait with you.'

They wait. The man changes from red to green, and they both start to walk across.

'Finally!'

Aleesha's belly audibly rumbles and she rubs it.

'How about you? What's your... how do you say... living situation?'

'I, uh, have my own place.'

Aleesha smiles and grabs Ben's baseball cap, and puts it on her head backwards. Ben looks at her, smiles, and doesn't say anything as they walk on.

'Have you got a girlfriend?'

'Nup.'

'Wow. Crazy.'

'What?!'

'Well. You know. You're....'

'What?!'

'Nothing.... What are you looking for?'

'I dunno. Just a real genuine girl I guess.'

'They're actually quite rare, you know?'

Aleesha smiles at Ben.

'Yeah.'

'And guys. Genuine guys. That have some... um... to them anyway.... What about you Ben. Are you a genuine guy?'

Ben blushes.

'You're blushing! You dork!'

Ben shakes his head whilst smiling and blushing. Aleesha shoulder bumps him. He looks at his arm where they bumped whilst smiling even more.

Ben walks to the low garden brick fence at the front of Sophie's house and sits nervously.

'This is Soph's.'

Aleesha joins Ben on the fence.

'Are we here too early?'

Ben takes his phone out and looks at the time.

'Nah. We're late.'

Aleesha smiles.

'Oh. Okay then.'

Ben smiles.

'I'm not sure I'm ready to....'

Ben nods towards the house. Aleesha smiles and smooths her hair. She looks at Ben while moistening her lips. He looks up and their eyes meet. They smile and avert their eyes.

'You're different Ben.'

'How?'

'I'm not sure yet!'

'Good different but?'

Aleesha nods. Ben smiles. They both look at the ground.

'Tell me something you haven't told anyone before?

'That's a funny one.'

'Come on, it'll be fun. Tell me a juicy secret so I'll know more about you.'

'Ummm.... I don't know hey. Ummm....'

'It's fine. You don't have to.'

'It's okay. It's a good question.... My parents want me to be... and I'm not sure I want to be, umm... an engineer.'

'Shit! I mean... um!'

Ben laughs.

'It's fine. I've said sugar honey ice and tea before!'

'I won't tell anyone I promise. Okay. Tell me more. You've started now.'

'My dad and grandad, and great grandad, are or were engineers, and I wanted to impress them.'

'But...?'

'I don't care about engineering. I mean... I'm sure it's okay.'

'What do you care about?'

'You're going to laugh at this.'

Aleesha smiles and waits.

'Art.'

'Art?'

'Art. You know... what you do.'

'Like drawing and stuff? But you said....'

'Yeah. I haven't done much since I was twelve, but I used to all the time before that.'

'I was wondering how you knew about Sheena. Why'd you stop?'

'To spend more time on maths and physics and chemistry and stuff. Getting to know my technical calculator.

'Yuck! Making good choices and all that.'

'Yeah. But I'm good at that stuff but.'

'What an awful problem to face Ben!'

Ben smiles.

'The struggle is real. Do you know who Rima is?'

'Again. Impressed. You know? I think I could help you with getting back into the art thingy.'

Ben smiles at Aleesha, and then this fades as he looks at Aleesha's eyes more intently.

'You know what? I think you could.'

Aleesha smiles.

'We'd better go in. We don't want to be rude and I'm not sure I've made a good impression on your mates yet!'

They head in as Aleesha checks her hair.

CHAPTER VII

Plenty

Missed opportunity

Aleesha and Ben walk through Sophie's kitchen past a table stacked with food which Aleesha surveys as she passes. Aleesha slows to a stop, and leans forwards to smell some garlic bread.

Ben stops behind Aleesha, and places his hand on the side of her hip, to keep her moving. Aleesha stops and straightens, while looking at Ben's hand. She turns and looks at him. She smiles and then bends down to have another sniff of the garlic bread, breathes in slowly with her eyes closed, and has a shiver of pleasure. Aleesha starts walking again and Ben lets his hand fall from her hip as she does so.

Ben opens the pool gate and they approach a table where Simon, Nick, Sophie, and Emma are sitting. Aleesha and

Ben accidentally bump shoulders, and look at each other and smile before looking away. Sophie watches this.

'There's plenty of food back there if you want some,' Simon advises.

'Great!' Aleesha rubs her tummy while everyone stares at her. Aleesha refocuses. She heads back through the pool gate as Ben takes a seat next to Simon. Sophie stands to follow Aleesha.

Sophie comes into the kitchen and pours herself a drink as Aleesha puts food on a plate. Sophie spills some juice which Aleesha notices so she grabs a towel and gives it to Sophie.

'That's a hand towel, not a dish cloth.'

'Sorry. Where's a dish cloth?' Aleesha asks.

'It's fine.'

Sophie heads towards a hallway with the hand towel. Charlotte who Aleesha hasn't noticed till now, comes up beside her. Charlotte puts some food on her plate as Aleesha finishes.

'Get it right Aleesha.'

'You!'

Aleesha's phone vibrates and she gets it out. She reads Kim's text message, 'Why won't you answer me?' Aleesha swipes to clear the message and turns vibrate off.

Charlotte sees that Aleesha's attention is back and adds, 'Sorry! Just teasing. I've seen you three times now.'

'Huh?'

'Church and the park, and now here.'

'You did? Huh. Didn't see you at church.'

'Yeah, I basically never go these days.'

Aleesha speaks in a quieter voice.

'And they still let you hang out with them?!'

Charlotte laughs.

'Yeah. You could say that. Some of them worry I'm going to hell because people who don't go to church every week automatically go to hell apparently.'

'Well then. I'm not sure I should be talking to you if you've got bad juju!'

Charlotte laughs.

Sophie reappears with a dish cloth and wipes up the juice and washes it in the kitchen sink. Sophie notices the amount of food on Aleesha's plate. 'Take it easy. The rest of us need to eat too.' Aleesha glances at the amount of food on the table and the number of people sitting out at the table by the pool. Sophie keeps walking out. Charlotte comes closer to Aleesha.

'I've got great juju thank you very much. I'm just not following the program the same as everyone else. That's all.'

'I don't think I am either... Too much food apparently.'

'Don't worry about it. Unless you're concerned about the approval of Ben's parents.'

'What?!'

'People talk.'

'Great.'

'You might want to dress better too. You know, brush your hair?'

Aleesha touches her hair, and looks at Charlotte.

'Shut up. You've been talking to Sophie.'

'Yep. Watch out for her. Being around Ben is risky business.'

Aleesha looks at Sophie who is watching them through the window from where she is sitting beside the pool.

'Huh? She's nothin. It must be a juju thing.'

Aleesha's phone in her pocket glows but she doesn't notice.

'Sorry. I'm probably not making any sense. Anyway. Don't worry. I'm sure everything will be fine.'

'Oh yeah. Is Tiana okay?'

Charlotte smiles.

'Yeah. She's awesome. She's okay. Thanks for checking on her though. I was impressed.'

Aleesha smiles. Charlotte looks at the amount of food on Aleesha's plate.

'You haven't eaten for a while?'

'Going my own way isn't going as easy as I'd hoped!'

'What do ya think about helping me out at the soup kitchen at the church tomorrow night?'

'Yeah, nah.'

'Are you sure? We really could use the help.'

'That sort of thing makes me really....'

Aleesha shivers and rubs her arms. She walks back to the others and Charlotte follows.

'Helping people?'

'Shut up! Mum's hard enough to sort out thanks and myself for that matter. I don't think I've got room for anyone else on the roster.'

Ben sees Aleesha and smiles at her. He pulls an empty chair closer to him. Aleesha's phone glows again, she gets her phone out and sees five missed calls from her mum.

Aleesha turns and runs to the pool gate and opens it. Sophie looks at the food that she's left behind. Nick turns to Ben.

'She had second thoughts mate?'

Aleesha comes into Rachel's hospital room at speed.

Rachel asks, 'What are you doing back here?'

'You called me like five times.'

'No I didn't.'

'Yeah you did.'

Aleesha gets her phone out. Rachel avoids looking at it.

'I don't know what you're trying to prove, but you can just fuck off.'

Aleesha looks towards the door, and leans a little towards it, which Rachel notices. Aleesha stops herself and looks down at her hand, that is rubbing her tummy.

'You said you were going to be here.'

'What?'

Aleesha turns back to face Rachel, who increases her volume.

'You said you were going to be here.'

Aleesha and Rachel raise their voices.

'I said I was going to be here?'

'Yeah. You did.'

'What?! That's the kettle....'

'You weren't here.'

'I'm here now so... stop living in the past. Honestly!'

'You weren't here when I needed, dumbass.'

'I was about to finally have something to eat... so shoot me!'

'Shut up Leesh. Don't go yelling at me. I wish I could go out and eat something.'

'I don't need this. I'm trying to sort shit out for myself like you said.'

'Oh. I'm sorry. You've got problems do you?'

'Yeah I do, and it's y.... Did you call Uncle Quade for me yet?'

'What happened to shacking up with mister teen heart throb?'

'He's... possibly worth the wai.... Shut up. I'm working on it, but I need somewhere to stay in the meantime so I can stop getting grass in my hair!'

'Why? What's the hold up little miss flirty?'

'His friends and maybe parents may need some more of my unique charm first....'

'You're just so wise, miss teen femme fatale!'

'Anyway. Did something happen or what?'

'Yes.'

'Yes what?'

'A silent ischaemia.'

'And...? What does that mean?'

'You didn't look anything up did you?'

'Come on. I didn't see anything about ischaemia having volume levels.'

'That's not funny Leesh. My heart just got more damaged... It was already screwed up, I don't need any more parts giving out on me.'

'Okay mum. Sorry. I shoulda been here. That sounds scary as shit.'

Rachel hardens. Aleesha turns and walks to the door.

'Sorry mum. I'll make it up to you.'

Rachel smiles and picks a banana up from her table and offers it to Aleesha. Aleesha stands looking at it.

CHAPTER VIII

Harden

Redirection

Aleesha sits on the grass at the back of the hospital, eating the banana. She starts to ponder her decision to make it by herself. She can't come up with a way of assessing this, so she falls back and quickly falls asleep.

Aleesha saunters into Rachel's room in the morning but Rachel doesn't see her. Rachel is perched on the other side of her bed from the doorway, with her feet treading the floor. A hospitality staff member, Louisa, starts to push the magazines and handbag to the side of the table so that she can put the meal tray down.

'Hey, hey, hey, hey, hey. What are you doing?'

Louisa stops and looks at Rachel.

'Sorry. What?'

'What do you think you're doing?'

Louisa steps back.

'Um. Sorry. I... I'm wanting to put your meal tray on the table.'

'Well don't just push my stuff out of the way.'

'Sorry.'

'Just ask me nicely, and I'll do it. I'm not dead yet.'

Rachel finishes making space for the meal tray. Louisa nervously places the meal tray down and pushes the table closer to Rachel, it accelerates quickly into Rachel's foot.

'Sorry!'

Aleesha looks like she feels the pain, and Rachel lets out a sharp breath of shock, and tries to clutch at her foot but isn't strong enough. She rubs her forehead strongly while gritting her teeth. Louisa removes the lid from the meal, pauses for a moment, looking at the food, then looks at Rachel nervously.

Aleesha sees Doctor Wilcox place a brown paper bag on the nurse's station, pick up an x-ray and then walk to look at it through a light. Aleesha leaves her mother's room and moves close to the bag. The staff are talking to each other or reading, and don't notice her grab it. Aleesha smiles at Louisa as they pass while Aleesha returns to her mother's room, but Louisa doesn't notice. Rachel looks up at Aleesha who hands her the bag.

'Here you go!'

Rachel looks in, and with a delighted look, pulls out a meat pie. She takes a big bite, and then stops before chewing and swallowing. But then does so quickly. She puts it down.

'I'm not feeling so good.'

Rachel begins to fumble around, trying to put a blanket over the back of her own shoulders, which she is finding difficult. She looks at Aleesha who is confused.

'Get that look off your face and help me. I'm cold.'

'What's wrong?'

'I dunno.'

Rachel looks irritated and in pain.

'Arrrhh... Okay then.'

Aleesha walks to the side of the bed where the cardiac monitors are, helps place a blanket over Rachel's shoulders. Rachel becomes more agitated and grabs the blanket with two hands either side of her chest and pulls it down strongly.

Cardiac monitors beep loudly and Aleesha gets out of the way as a nurse rushes to Rachel, pulls the emergency latch that flattens the bed and Rachel is sucked back into the bed and bounces from the impact. Three other nurses rush into the room. One nurse is pushing the cardiac resuscitation trolley at speed, another rushes to the monitor and turns the alarm off, and the other one joins the first nurse at the head of the bed.

Aleesha sinks back against the wall as this is happening. She comes to, and then walks to the door.

Aleesha rings Ben. Sophie sees Aleesha's name on Ben's phone while he is swimming with Emma and Simon. Sophie looks up at Ben who is wrestling Simon and she quickly hangs up on Aleesha.

'Here I come Benny,' she lets out with a delighted squeal.
Sophie drops her towel and runs for the pool.

Aleesha enters the church the next night and approaches
Charlotte who is setting the tables. Other people are in
the background cooking large pots of food.

'You came!'

'Sorry. Do you still want help?'

'Of course!'

'Today was shii... bad, and even if you have....'

'I don't. Really! I don't. How's your mum?'

'I don't want to think about her for a while.'

'Um.'

'Yeah.... I can just be so, so stupid, sometimes.... If you
had've told me a couple of days ago my mum had died?
I wouldn't have even blinked.... But I don't think I'm
ready for all that.'

'Are you hungry?'

'Yes, yes, yes.'

'Cool. We eat last.'

Charlotte starts to walk and looks at Aleesha to follow.

'This is one of my dad's dreams. He finally got this going
a few months ago. Hey dad. Come meet Aleesha.'

Lou walks to them.

'Thanks for helping out. We're normally run off our feet
in here.'

'Hey. No worries.'

58

Lou smiles and returns to carrying the dishes from the stove to the serving bench.

Charlotte continues, 'The church board kept getting in the way, and even though he's got this far, they give him, like less than a dollar per person.'

One of the other helpers hands Charlotte a big basket of bread rolls.

'You must have to spend heaps!'

'Yeah well. We know God wants us to, so we do. The place will fill up soon. You wanna serve with me?'

'Sure.'

Aleesha follows Charlotte to serve as a queue forms. Aleesha enjoys playing her role and seeing the appreciation on people's faces.

Aleesha hands the last dish to Charlotte, who dries it and puts it away. They walk to the side door with two plastic plates of food that they have eaten some of the food from. Aleesha follows Charlotte who sits on the side of the road and joins her.

A lady locks the front door of the church, waves at the girls as she leaves, and they wave back.

Aleesha pulls her phone out of her pocket. She texts Ben, 'Do you want to hang out at yours tomorrow?'

Ben texts a reply, 'Do you want to come to Soph's tomorrow at 7?'

Aleesha rolls her eyes.

'Does no one else have a house that they can hang out at?'

'What?'

'Sophie. Why do they always gotta go to hers?'

'Dunno. It's what they've always done I guess.'

'Makes it freakin hard to get anywhere but!'

Aleesha returns her attention to her phone and she replies with, 'Sure.' Aleesha puts her phone back in her pocket.

'How'd ya go in there?' Charlotte asks.

'You guys are really good!'

Aleesha yawns and Charlotte yawns as well. Aleesha notices and laughs at Charlotte, who laughs as well.

'All the things that I normally think about are starting to come back into my head now... and I didn't miss them!'

'Well then, tell 'em to piss off!'

'Language Charlotte! Yeah, see?... There is a bit of fire in you!'

'I've got good juju I swear!'

'That's not what Sophie was saying!'

'What?'

'Nothing. I was just....'

'What's she been saying?'

'Really. Nothing. I was, I was just teasing.'

'Great. Good one. It wouldn't be the first time is all.... I've been wondering... what's it like looking after your mum?'

'I wish she'd stop dying every second day! Really freakin inconvenient to getting past this, like, being stuck. Moth to a flame... even though I wish every night that I'd flown in the other direction.'

Aleesha approaches her mum who is sitting up and eating.

'You scared the crap out of me yesterday.'

'I didn't enjoy it either.'

Aleesha approaches the bed.

'Was that a noisy one?'

Rachel starts to sob.

'I'm....'

Aleesha's eyes brim with tears.

'You still sleeping out the back?'

'Yep.'

'You're really rockin your independent streak aren't you?!'

'I'll get there.'

'Not by yourself you won't.'

Aleesha is confused.

'Matthew was here earlier. He's cancelled your placement.'

Aleesha shrugs her shoulders.

'He said to call a crisis shelter if you want somewhere....'

'Fuck that! The people at those places are dangerous as fuck! You know what?'

Rachel doesn't respond.

'I think I've successfully exited care early. Didn't fuckin expect that! Ah well. Fuck them and all their, "oh Aleesha, you're so bad, we're going to go and hide from you." Stupid fuckers.'

'Yeah well. Lucky for you, I've decided that you can go to Quade's.'

'Really?! Well what do you know?'

'Don't get carried away Leesh. You'll understand when you're older. And what happened with that boy you were seducing anyway?'

Aleesha rolls her eyes.

'He's not even real is he? You made that shit up to try to fool me into thinking that you got smarts, hey?!'

'He is so fuckin real. You'll see.'

CHAPTER IX

Family

Thicker than water

Aleesha is walking with her skateboard and bag down a street. She passes a childcare centre and stops to look in. She smiles as a little girl does a forward roll. Aleesha searches for the childcare workers. She spots them drinking coffee inside. The girl she was watching falls. Aleesha looks at the workers. She waits, and then kicks the fence as they don't respond. Aleesha leaves.

Aleesha walks up the driveway of an expensive large two level house in dense suburbia and knocks on the door. Quade who is in his forties opens the door.

'Quade mate!'

'Hi. Sorry. Um... I'm sorry, but, do I know you?'

'Your niece.'

'No you're not! Leesh is like this tiny little thing.' Gestures height of toddler.

'She was. Are you saying I'm fat now?!'

'Yeah, no. Not getting into that. One of the benefits of experience. So how are you? You look great... and so grown up!'

'Thanks.'

'You look just like your mum. Wait... Do you know...?'

'Yeah. She said I could come and see you.'

'Do you have somewhere to stay?'

'Nup. Not yet. I was hopi....'

'How about you bunk with me, for old times sake?'

'Umm. Stay... for a couple of days while I work on getting my own place... would be awesome. Thanks!'

Quade walks inside. Aleesha follows. He stops and turns and to her. Aleesha stops to maintain the distance between them.

'You know, I really should've recognized you. You look exactly like your mum used to!'

Quade is staring at Aleesha (looking her up and down) while smiling, and Aleesha is smiling back, but her smile fades and she rubs her arms.

'Let me take your bag.'

Aleesha pulls her bag a bit closer to herself.

'Okay, you bring it. Come on up.'

Quade beckons and he leads the way up the stairs. Aleesha follows Quade into the room, and walks past him. She stops and looks past him back out the door, and then meets his gaze, and tries to look confident.

'Your mum was staying in here. Here's a key to the front door. Help yourself to anything in the kitchen you want, and let me know if I can do anything for you. Anything at all that you want.'

'I want mum....'

'To get some chill?'

'Pretty close, I'm impressed!'

'Your mum and I have met! She isn't the easiest.... Sometimes I was the only other person in the world for her. The rest of the time, and all the time now, I'm less important than the grit under her shoes.'

'Yep. That's mum. I'm hoping she... chills a bit and learns to listen a bit. Before she karks it, that is.'

Aleesha tenses the muscles in her upper body which Quade looks over. Quade smiles as he is looking at parts of her body other than her face. Their eyes meet.

'Anyway. I'm popping out but I'll be back later.'

Aleesha starts to walk in the front entrance of the hospital. She stops, turns around, and walks back out as she decides that she just isn't up for it right now.

Ben is sitting on the brick fence at the front of Sophie's house as Aleesha arrives.

'I was wondering if you'd turn up.'

'Have you been stood up before have you Ben?!'

They sit.

'No. But I don't normally worry this much.'

Aleesha playfully pushes Ben.

'Stop it.'

Ben laughs.

'I worried about you when you ran off.'

'It's all good. It was just my mum.'

'Yeah? You two close?'

'She's awful... actually... that topic's not on the menu.'

'Okay.'

'What about you?'

'Me and my parents?'

'Yeah.'

'They're really hard to deal with.'

'Really?'

'No. They're awesome!'

Aleesha play hits Ben.

'What's that like?'

'It's not always good. Sometimes they're annoying.'

'How?'

'Like dad makes me make my own decisions, and won't just tell me what to do.'

'Wow. What a bas...'

'Yeah I know. But sometimes I really don't know what to do.'

Aleesha realizes that Sophie is standing behind them, but Sophie doesn't smile at Aleesha. She looks at Ben who hasn't turned around yet.

'Are you coming in Benny?' Sophie asks.

Ben turns around quickly and stands. Sophie disappears. Ben and Aleesha head in.

Ruth approaches Aleesha and Ben in the kitchen.

'Are you going to introduce us?'

'Sure. Aleesha. This is Ruth, Sophie's mum. She's the best cook. After my mum that is!'

'Hey.'

'Great to meet you! You kids go on and have fun!'

Aleesha smiles and moves past the food, and starts to lean in to some garlic bread. She sees Ben come close behind her, and raise his hand to put on her hip. She dodges his hand, grabs the whole garlic bread and runs ahead of him laughing.

Nick, Emma, Sophie and Simon are sitting on the edge of the pool. Simon is driving a remote controlled yacht. Ben and Aleesha join them. Aleesha starts to eat the garlic bread with occasional groans of pleasure. Sophie watches. 'Awwwwhhoorrr. Hell yeah.' Aleesha looks up to see everyone else looking at her.

'You right there?' Sophie asks.

'Yeah yeah yeah. Thanks. Carry on.'

Ben reaches for one of the pieces of garlic bread that Aleesha is holding. Aleesha moves so as not to be in the Sophie's line of sight. Aleesha bares her teeth at Ben and gives a soft growl.

'Ggggrrrrr!'

Ben withdraws his hand.

Sophie picks up where she left off 'Where was I? ...Oh yeah. That's right. So this lady has like missing teeth with matted hair and really, really dirty clothes down by the train station. I tried to help her by picking up her grubby bags, you know? To get them under the cover of the station, and out of the rain. But she started swearing at me.'

'Why did she do that?' Nick asks.

Aleesha puts the garlic bread wrapper down, and rests her hands behind her, with one of her hands near Ben's hand.

'I dunno. I mean that was all she had in the world I think, and it needed to stay dry,' Sophie responds.

Ben moves his hand closer to Aleesha's. She looks at him, smiles, then places her hand on top of his. Ben smiles and stays looking ahead.

'What'd ya do?' Nick asks.

Aleesha hears this and looks at Sophie.

'I said, listen here lady. I'm trying to help you. But she just kept on swearing at me and waving her finger in my face. But I couldn't really make out what she was saying.'

'That's mean,' Emma contributes.

Aleesha's eyebrows furrow.

'I know. I felt really sad. I can't understand it. Anyway. So I'm writing a skit for church, where the woman keeps going back to try to help, and eventually the homeless lady becomes friendly, and apologizes because she comes to realize that I was just trying to help her.'

'So awesome,' Emma says with excitement.

'Thanks!'

'Can I be in it?' Emma asks.

'Yaa-uh! I'll do your makeup and you'll look stunning!'

Aleesha has continued to have furrowed eyebrows. She looks at Ben, and he gently shakes his head but she decides to go ahead.

'Maybe she just didn't want you touching her stuff?'

Everyone turns to look at her, but Ben looks back in front of him, and quickly retracts his hand to himself.

Nick lets out a 'Wooooo!'

Aleesha looks at Ben questioningly, but he stares straight ahead, and adjust his posture from side to side.

'What's your problem?' Sophie asks.

'Sophie!' Simon says out of surprise.

Aleesha looks at Sophie.

'No Simon. If she's gonna give it out, she better be able to take it. Aleesha. Is there something you want to say?'

'Easy Soph,' Simon pleads.

'I'm not sure. I mean. There's a lot to explain. What actual helping looks like, respect of other people's belongings, personal spa....'

'Oh no you didn't. You didn't just come in to my house and eat my food, and think that you can talk to me like that?'

'Well... I spose I did. Because I just did.'

Simon crashes the yacht into the pool wall and it sinks.

Sophie lets out a scream, 'Simon! That's my dad's. He's going to kill me.'

'I can fix it,' Simons adds hastily.

Simon grabs the boat and takes it to the house in a rush.

Sophie turns to Ben.

'Ben. Is there anything you want to say to your new friend?'

Ben avoids eye contact. Aleesha looks at him. Aleesha gets up and starts to leave.

Aleesha passes Simon as she's leaving through the kitchen and he turns off the hair dryer from drying the yacht.

'You're not leaving are you?'

'Uhhh.... Yep. That I am.'

'Oh sorry. She has a good heart. She doesn't mean any harm.'

Aleesha looks exhausted and turns to leave as Simon turns the hair dryer on again.

CHAPTER X

Introductions

More than meets the eye

Ben catches up to Aleesha as she is trying to open the front gate. She is having difficulty, so she kicks it with a strong kick and it breaks off.

Aleesha picks up the gate and tries nervously to play back in a way that it will stay standing. Ben is watching but Aleesha doesn't see him. She props the gate against the wall and heads down the street.

Ben catches up to Aleesha and he falls into step beside her.

'I'm surprised you came. But now that you have. What was that Ben?'

'What?'

'Like my job is to keep my mouth shut while she.... Calling her Captain clueless would be....'

Aleesha stops, and Ben stops as well.

Aleesha glares at him. Ben isn't making eye contact so he doesn't notice.

'I'm sure you two can get on, if you spend more time together to find what you have in common. She's a good person really.'

Aleesha starts walking again, and Ben does as well.

'No matter how many times you guys says that – it doesn't make it true. Anyway... what did she do to Charlotte?'

'What do you mean?'

'Charlotte seems traumatized by her.'

'Uh. Yeah? I dunno hey.'

'You must know something. All you guys are tight little peas in a pod.'

'Yeah. Charlotte is too.... Well maybe not now. I guess she's not around as.... Anyway, how's your mum?'

'That's where I'm going now. I haven't let her have some of my... yet, but I'm close.'

'You okay?'

Aleesha takes a big breath, then looks at her tummy.

'You're a massive dork, but maybe that's why you're so adorable.'

Ben blushes.

'Ermmm... thanks. Did you know that while women are more empathetic than men, only about 10% of the variance is from genetic variations?'

'Uuhhhhhh. No. Um. Do you want to be my wingman with mum?'

'Why?'

'Give you a chance to redeem yourself?'

'Weren't you saying that she's a bit....'

'She's mostly just hot air, and don't hold her against me okay? She's not my fault.'

Ben nods tentatively.

Ben buys flowers from the hospital gift shop which is about to shut while Aleesha waits.

'Are you ready?' Aleesha asks.

Ben looks uncertain.

'She loves flowers so I'm sure she will love you. Just don't go quoting any of those things that come out of you when you're nervous.'

Aleesha strolls to Rachel's bed, holding Ben behind her. Rachel looks green and ill.

'I knew you were dying to meet him, so....'

Rachel looks sharply at Aleesha.

Ben hands flowers to Rachel. Rachel fixes her hair. Ben tries to summon a charming smile.

'It's great to meet you!'

'Why's that?'

Rachel takes the flowers and throws them in bin gently as her strength fades easily.

'Way to make an impression mum!'

Rachel turns to Ben.

'So, how are you going Ben? Have I scared you off?'

Ben looks unsure.

'No maam....'

'Maam?! Wow. Where'd you find this guy?! Oh yeah. Church.'

'Great memory mum. You're on a roll.'

'Ben. Come a bit closer now and sit here beside me, so that I don't have to keep straining to look up at you.'

Ben gets a chair and moves it closer to the bed and sits. Aleesha stands beside him.

'Don't worry. I won't bite.'

Ben moves his chair a bit closer.

'Yes mm.... Yes. Sure.'

'Oooh, he can learn just like Quade di....'

Rachel's eyes meets Aleesha's and Rachel quickly turns back to Ben who is blushing.

'That's right Ben. Don't call me maam.'

'No worries. Did you know that heart disease is the leading single cause of death in Australia.... About 20,000 people die a year from it.'

'Thanks Ben.... Very helpful....'

Rachel rolls her eyes. She looks at Aleesha.

'He does seem oddly real... Hmmm. Maybe really o....'

'Great observation mum.'

'Ben. I've got one question for you.'

'Yes?'

'Why did you come to meet me?'

Aleesha looks at Ben who turns to her as well. Aleesha tries to help out.

'I'm not sure this question has a correct answer, so don't worry about it.'

'Well Aleesha mentioned you, and she invited....'

Rachel suddenly doubles over in pain, then bangs her hand into her chest, where her heart is, and then slaps her other hand over the top of it, pulling in and arching her back as she lets out a loud groan.

Ben is horrified and he starts to raise his hand, as if to call out for help. Rachel has her eyes shut but then opens one to look at Ben who is looking to the doorway. She sits up.

'I'm just playing.'

Ben looks at Rachel, scratches his head. He looks at Aleesha questioningly. Rachel turns to Aleesha.

'He's not too bright this one. Watch out for that.'

Ben looks angry.

'You're doing a great job looking out for me mum!'

'Huh?! Yeah well you should appreciate what I'm doing for you here. Your mumma knows more than you think.'

'Come on Ben. Let's go. I'm tired.'

'Are you still at Quade's?' Rachel asks.

'Yeah.... Why?'

'How's that going for you?'

'Why?'

Rachel looks away.

'Okay then.'

Aleesha walks out of the room. Ben follows and he looks back over his shoulder at Rachel.

'Nice to meet you!'

'Piss off numbnuts,' Rachel says in annoyance.

CHAPTER XI

Pleasure

Who benefits?

Aleesha walks out the front door of the hospital and Ben follows her out.

'I think that's the first time I've seen her dislike someone more than me. That was fun! Maybe my magic charm ain't on the blink after all.'

'Your mother... is.... I don't the name... because I've... never seen anyone as....'

Aleesha waits anxiously.

'Okay. I almost... well... slapped her... but I didn't want to touch her, you know what I mean?'

'Really?'

'I've never even met her before, and she's treating me like that? I bought her flowers for heaven's sake.'

'What the hell?'

'What?'

'You're not serious?'

'I am. I was wondering why you didn't seem that nice about her... but now.'

'Well I am nice to her and what's wrong with you? You're a Christian for Pete's sake!'

'What? Oh sorry. You're right. She's your mum.... I got a bit.... You're right. You're right. Sorry.... Why didn't you worry about the whole clutching her chest back there?'

'We know each other.... That and no alarms went off.'

'Ahhh.'

'Anyway, I'm beat. I'm turning in. See you at the skate park tomorrow?'

Ben hesitates.

'Uh.... The guys were going to head to the park.'

'Why?!'

'I dunno.... We do pretty much everything together before the holidays are over I guess.'

'Okay. But, can you take me out after, like, just me?!'

'Um. Yeah? Where do you want to go?'

'I hear Picnic Point can be romantic?'

Ben smiles.

Aleesha comes happily through the door to Rachel's room.

'Where is he?'

'Gone home.'

'I was waiting for him to try to convert me. Was piss weak though.'

'At least they look after me a little... unlike some people....'

'That's not my job you little brat. You can just fuck off back to Matthew.'

'What?'

Rachel imitates Aleesha by repeating what she said in an exaggerated way.

'What?'

Aleesha shakes off the impact of this.

'Anyway. I thought you were doing a good job of checking him out.'

'Oh honey. That wasn't for you. I just think he's a floppy nubile dickwad.'

'Have you ever come even a little close to being... like... not like there's a super charged rod of iron up your arse because it's obviously taking a toll. I mean look at you.'

'Come closer and you'll find out. I assure you.'

'Oh, I know. Coming closer isn't going to help me learn anything new.'

They stare at each other. Aleesha averts her eyes and then leaves.

Aleesha walks past the nurses desk. Doctor Wilcox sees her and catches up to her.

'Just thought I'd let you know that you may want to take it easy on your mum. Her body is really close to giving up on her.'

Aleesha eyes him for a while.

'I get the feeling that she'd punch death in the face if it turned up, so I'm not worried about her.'

'Yeah. She's....'

'Yeah she is.'

'She's strong. But that intensity is what's going to kill her. When she gets worked up, not enough blood is getting to her heart which makes it not function properly.'

'I'll say.'

'This is serious Aleesha. She has so much plaque in her arteries, and she has already had a number of times when this has come away, and a blood clot has formed, stopping blood from getting to her heart. The next time is going to kill her.'

Aleesha looks at Doctor Wilcox, and loses focus on him.

'Aleesha?'

Aleesha regains focus, and her eyes moisten. She walks away.

Quade is hunched over his phone on the couch. He looks up to see Aleesha get a drink from the fridge, and he quickly puts his phone face down on the couch beside him.

'Is it okay if I have a shower?'

'Yes! Of course. You know where, hey?'

Aleesha nods.

'Thanks.'

Aleesha heads upstairs. Aleesha sees two sets of shampoo and conditioner as she showers, one for women and one for men. Aleesha finishes, looks in a bathroom draw, and sees pads and a hair dryer. She blow dries her hair.

Aleesha approaches Quade who is playing on his phone.

'Uncle Quade?'

'Just Quade will do. Yeah?'

'Did dad and you get on good with pops and ma?'

'Your dad didn't. He was a fighter. I'm more of a lover.'

'Did pops and ma look after you?'

'Of course. I'm very lovable. Why are you asking?'

'Um…. I'm beginning to doubt that I can make it… without help.'

'How do you mean?'

'People aren't being as useful as…. I'm beginning to wonder how helpful Ben is planning on being.'

'Don't worry about a thing Leeshy. Come. Come. Sit.'

Quade pats the couch next to him, and puts on a charming smile. Aleesha sits next to him, while he is staring at her.

'Selfie?'

Quade puts his arm around Aleesha and takes a picture that she does a half smile for. He leaves his arm around her as he puts the phone in his pocket. She shrugs his arm off.

'Quade?'

'Yeah?'

'Thanks for letting me stay here, even if it's only for a few days. I really appreciate it….'

'The pleasure is truly mine.'

Quade puts his arm around Aleesha for a hug which she accepts, but she adjusts her posture on looking at him holding her tighter. Quade straightens a strand of her hair.

'What's wrong with my hair?'

'Nothing! You're great, and a great looking girl Aleesha.'

His hand slides down her back to her bottom and starts to squeeze. Aleesha stands, shaken.

'Um. I can't take any more excitement today. I think I'm gonna go to bed.'

'To bed?'

'Yep. Once I'm through the door I'll be gone.'

Aleesha walks to the stairs and Quade watches her go, considering whether or not to follow her.

CHAPTER XII

Unleash

Values collide

Aleesha falls on the bed in Quade's spare room. She turns and lies on her back. She hears Quade leave the house, waits for a while, gets up slowly, and listens, and then goes to open the door. She walks to Quade's bedroom door. After a pause she moves into the room.

Aleesha feels her way to Quade's bed. She gets her phone out, and turns the screen before deciding to risk turning the bedroom light on.

She walks to the drawers, opens them, and sees male and female underwear. She opens another draw and pulls out a jumper. Out of it falls a picture of Rachel on Quade's lap. Her jaw drops, and she puts it back quickly and shuts the draw and moves quickly to leave the room.

Aleesha goes back to the spare room and pulls the door shut.

She jumps into bed, pulling the covers over her, and breathing heavily before settling.

She tries to piece together what her mum meant by asking her about how staying with Quade is working out. Aleesha startles, walks to the door, and sits on the floor with her back against it.

She doses off but wakes again when she hears a gentle knock on her door. She looks beside her and sees shadows under the door from feet and smells alcohol radiating from what she assumes is Quade's breathing. She pushes back harder against the door. The shadows get narrower. Aleesha takes a big breath before putting her hand on her chest to feel her heart rate. She hears Quade's bedroom door shut.

The next morning Aleesha is sitting on the couch eating some toast. She jumps when she sees Quade standing in the doorway looking at her.

'What were you doing in my room?' he asks.

'Why would I go into your room?'

'That's what I'm asking you.'

'Doesn't sound like asking.'

Quade moves closer and she leans backwards to get further away from him.

'I'm not going to ask again.'

'I thought you wanted me in your room.'

'Nice try. What were you looking for?'

'Nothing.'

'Yeah you were.'

84

'Why? Are you trying to hide something Quade?'

Quade straightens.

'That's it, isn't it. They're mum's clothes in your draws and you've been trying to pop her daughter, and your niece, as well.'

Quade's posture relaxes and he grins.

'And you're not making it easy you fucking slut.'

Aleesha bristles, stands and walks menacingly towards Quade.

'Coz I'm not my mum, and I have no fucking intention of being her. For you, or anyone, you miserably pathetic fuckwit.'

Aleesha pushes past Quade and grabs her skateboard and bag.

Aleesha rides her skateboard up to Charlotte at the skate park.

'Do you ever get that hairs on the back of your neck, you're about to scratch some deep dark red, and spurting bloody lines into someone's face and chest kind of feeling?'

Charlotte grimaces.

'Not that exact feeling. No. Your mum?'

'No. Well, yes. But no. But I need to make good choices! If I don't explode in a torrent of frenzied apocalypsed retribution on their... arses in the meantime. Dad would've turned in his grave. I wonder if he was still alive when....' Aleesha shudders.

'That's it. Let it out.'

'You don't want that Charlotte. No one wants that.'

Aleesha approaches and drops in at the skate bowl while Charlotte watches with surprise. Ben and Simon arrive and sit on the nearby seesaw. Sophie and Emma arrive. Sophie stops when she sees Aleesha, and then looks over to see Ben smiling at Aleesha. Aleesha sees Charlotte fold her arms upon noticing that Sophie has arrived.

Aleesha is smiling as she skates. Charlotte and Ben watch her as she is staying focused on skating with occasional glances at them. Aleesha stops to rest, and Charlotte approaches her.

'You're freakishly good!'

'Thanks! I needed to clear my head…. I'm still having trouble figuring out you and your bad juju in this group but!'

Charlotte looks pained.

'How come you hang out with them?' Charlotte asks.

Aleesha shrugs her shoulders.

'Just because I keep hanging out with them, doesn't mean it doesn't suck. Like I overheard one of them the other day, say that the reason they go to church, is to remind them not to be a dickhead. And I was like, you might wanna try something else, coz it ain't working!'

Sophie comes within earshot.

'Sophie could use some help, and I'd thought she'd be the one who'd be helping me,' Aleesha says.

'Great. You're really getting to know her!' Charlotte replies.

'I'm the one who needs help?!'

Aleesha and Charlotte grimace, and turn to face Sophie who is walking closer to them.

'You still haven't even sorted out your hair.'

Aleesha goes to check her hair and then stops herself. Ben and Simon come a little closer, and Emma joins Sophie.

'And you. You would side with her wouldn't you?' Sophie directs at Charlotte.

'That's just like you. Always thinking that there are sides,' Charlotte replies.

'Shut up. Now you.'

Sophie closes the space between her and Aleesha.

'Have you got anything else smart to say to me?'

'Well I could try.... But I fear it would be wasted....'

Sophie steps in closer, and Aleesha doesn't move.

'Okay smarty. Try this. You shouldn't bite the hand that feeds you.'

'That's all you've got? You feed me?'

'Why else do you come around?'

Aleesha looks at Ben. Ben looks at the ground.

'Ben?' Sophie asks.

Aleesha reluctantly looks back at Sophie.

'Here we go,' Aleesha says.

'Damn right. Why the hell would he want a pathetic hobo bogan trailer trash piece of scum like you apart from pity for your embarrassing ass?'

'We could check his thoughts if they plan on coming out any time soon?' Aleesha responds.

'Great!' Sophie says.

They both turn to Ben. He doesn't look up.

'He wouldn't say anything to you, because he's too nice. But we've all agreed that you're not good enough for him. You freeloading give it out, but can't take it grub.'

Aleesha rolls her eyes and turns and starts to leave. Sophie grabs Aleesha's shoulder and then gets in front of her, with their chests almost touching. She raises her voice.

'Oh no you don't. You don't treat me like I'm not important.'

'Don't touch me. You don't want what comes with that.'

Sophie pushes up against Aleesha.

'I'm warning you,' Aleesha says.

Aleesha has a strong stance, clenches her fist and rocks back, looking ready to swing but looks at Ben and then steels herself. Sophie whispers.

'Ben's finished his charity kick with you, and these are my friends. You're on your own sweetheart. Aren't you? It's just you. And. Well. No one. No one worth a damn anyway.'

Aleesha looks at Ben and he is looking at the ground. Sophie raises her voice.

'And your drawings are worse than my 3 year old nephew's crayon scribbles. Isn't that what you said Ben?'

Aleesha looks at Ben in shock.

'Yeah. You heard me. You're nothing, and the fact you think you are, would make it even funnier, if you weren't so tragic.... Time to go sweetheart.'

Aleesha looks at Ben, shakes her head, and gently pushes past Sophie's shoulder as she leaves, tears falling.

After she passes, Sophie leans forwards and takes in a deep dramatic breath.

'She's really damaged goods that one.'

Sophie looks at Ben while still bent over as she says this. Charlotte approaches Sophie who sees this but doesn't look up at her.

'It's okay. Charlotte. I'm all good.'

Charlotte escalates, 'I'm not here to check on you!'

Charlotte kicks Sophie hard in the shins and Sophie drops to the ground. Charlotte leans over her.

'Are you all good now?'

Charlotte storms off.

Simon approaches Sophie who is sat on the ground rubbing her shins with Emma fussing over her.

'Um…. Soph…. I'm not sure that was what we're….'

Emma stops him, 'Not now Simon.'

Sophie watches Charlotte who is leaving the park onto the road.

CHAPTER XIII

Questions

Painful vulnerability

Aleesha is a couple of streets away by now. She stops and gets her phone. She texts Ben, 'I'm at the corner of North and James. Meet me?'

Ben tentatively approaches Aleesha who is pacing.

'You're getting into a bit of a habit here Ben.'

'She did have a point…. Were you, um… getting to know me because I've got money, and you're, you're, well homeless?'

'Um…. Well. I really could do with some help, yes.'

'Are you serious?'

'Uhhhhhh. Yep.'

'Why doesn't that embarrass you?'

'Why does it embarrass you?'

'You're in care. The government looks after you, right?'

Aleesha makes a 'sort of' gesture.

'Are you even from the Gold Coast?'

'Withcott.'

'Wow. You're something…. I've been wondering since I met your mum…. Are you any better than her?'

Aleesha freezes.

'Because you seem like you think you are, but from here….'

Aleesha scratches at the ground with her foot for a few beats and starts to get tears in her eyes.

'So, being helpful isn't your bag?'

'You're just not….'

Aleesha looks behind her, she looks at Ben, turns, and leaves.

Aleesha walks down the hallway and passes a body bag on a hospital. Aleesha quickens her pace. Aleesha rushes into Rachel's room. Rachel is looking even more haggard.

'Hey love. You ready to give it up yet and get your butt back in care?'

'Uh, no?!'

'Right. So you enjoyed the attention from dickwad?'

'I don't know.'

'You give up the goods?'

'What are you talking about? Ben's just a lily-livered useless fucktard is all.'

'Ben? Oh right. Ben. What happened?'

'Sophie was all up in my face.'

'What?'

'Yep.'

'What'd you do?'

'I punched her.'

'Who?'

'Sophie. Try to keep up.'

'Gimme five.'

Aleesha gives a gentle high-five as Rachel is looking frail.

'What else could you do? I would've liked to have seen that. How come you didn't tell me? I would've come and watched.'

'Sorry I didn't book you in. Nah... I couldn't do it. Ben was watching.'

'That's a shame. It could have actually been fun hanging around you.'

'And you're a cup of laughs twenty-four seven aren't you?!'

'Well you can't win'em all. But I say what I mean, and I mean what I say.'

'Yeah yeah mum, you're my hero. Even if you are dying.'

'Thanks Leesh. I can die happy now that my daughter respects me. You're much, much, more like me than you know, and....'

Aleesha stays standing for a while with a glazed look.

'Why did you stop coming to see me?'

'Give me a break Leesha.'

'Why didn't you want to see me? Like back then? I was still little and... not like I am now?'

'It was easier not to see you.'

'Seeing me would have been too much effort?'

'Yeah it was. It'd get me thinking about your dad. It was easier to stay home,'

'What about me though?'

'He blamed me for you being taken.'

'But what if I wanted to see you? Why couldn't that register?'

'That's why he left me, and ended up getting sick and dying. That's all because of you. I didn't do that to him.'

'No. Another big cup of not my fault.'

'Nah, yeah it was.'

'You're not right in the head.'

'I told you not to tell anyone.'

'Not tell anyone what?'

'You told Quade about dad punching you in the head.'

'Did I? Well fuck me. I'm pretty sure Quade saw enough with his own eyes. I doubt I would've said shit to him. I was too fucking small.'

'He said you did.'

'He says a lot of shit... and you two....'

'He had a crack… didn't he?!'

'What? You knew… he was going to do that?'

'He's Quade. He was useful for a bit of, you know. Even though he think's it's his charm. He does like'em young though. Always has. I used to have to dress….'

'What the fuck? How could you do that to me?'

'You needed to smarten up and get back to where you were. I was doing you a favour.'

'I lied. I didn't just leave. They were about to kick me out and not give me a place to go, so I left a little early to save the embarrassment is all.

'And came to me? Still rackin my brain on that one.'

'You're so… so dense.'

'Pot calling the kettle…. Have you ever stopped to think about me, how much stress I was and am under, and everything you've done to me? Let's not fuckin forget about that.'

'Ah, wow. What did I ever do to you? I was eight. What the fuck did you want from an eight year old?'

'I expected you to keep your fucking mouth shut, like I fucking told you.'

'You're fucked. Dad used to hit you too, you stupid fuck.'

'And I hit you too, but not e–fucking–nuff as it turns out.'

'Yep. Fuck you. I don't care how much anyone can whip me. It ain't going to mean you get control…. Fuck! That felt really good to say. I'm still fucking me!'

'Yeah well. You don't have me.'

'And I don't want you, you useless….'

'All I can say is you're your father's daughter.'

'And that's supposed to be an insult?'

'Do what you like.'

'Thanks for your permission, but I was going to anyway. Of course I'm my father's daughter. That's fucking logical. And I'm your daughter, you stuuuupiiiiiddd cow.'

'Nup. I'm done with you. What makes you think you can talk to me like this?'

'Because I fucking am. Why do people ask me such fucking obvious questions...? I'm so tired of your bullshit. For the longest time I wanted you to be the tiniest bit fucking useful, and parent the fuck up. But no. I got you. I don't like it, but what the fuck can I do?'

'And what could I do about having you? I never wanted you, so stop putting your bullshit on me.'

'Course you didn't, coz you're utterly fucked in the head.'

Rachel turns her back on Aleesha and Aleesha takes a big breath.

Aleesha continues, 'I can't say I feel better, but I'm sure as shit pleased to give back to you what's stored up in me because of you.... I don't see why the fuck I should suffer with it all by myself, when you're the one who fucking put it there. You fucked-up mum. Not me. So in summary... fuck you, and fuck you for making me fucked up too.'

Aleesha storms out.

CHAPTER XIV

Silence

Sinking below the surface

Aleesha is skating at the skate park with more physicality than usual and feeling relieved that the place is now mostly deserted.

She sits on the edge of the skate bowl next to her bag, breathing rapidly. Aleesha's phone rings, and she answers. 'Oh. Hey Kim.... Yeah I know. I've had a lot going on.... Yep yep.... What?... That's awful. Fuuuuck. That sucks man. Sorry. I always liked him.... Yep. Sorry. You okay?... Yeah. But not yet. I've got too much going on.... Kim, not now.' Aleesha hangs up and she sinks to the ground in a daze.

Aleesha's phone rings again. Aleesha answers. Aleesha hangs up and takes off as fast as she can go.

Aleesha walks past the nurses desk at speed. A nurse who is at the desk calls out to her, and Aleesha turns around. The nurse walks up to Aleesha and talks in a low, quiet voice.

'I've increased your mum's pain medication. She may understand you, but she probably won't be able to respond. It's hard to say exactly how long she has left, but it probably won't be long. She won't be in any pain.'

Aleesha pauses to try and take it all in.

Aleesha approaches Rachel's bed, and sits beside her, taking her hand.

'Mum?'

Rachel's eyes are closed and they flicker.

'Mum? You're not actually going to stay quiet and listen this time?!'

Aleesha takes a long moment where her amused expression fades, and sadness washes over her. She gets tears in her eyes. She continues to sit beside her mum for hours.

Aleesha is asleep on a chair beside the bed. She wakes and holds Rachel's hand. Aleesha's attention focuses on Rachel's chest, and she realizes that it is no longer moving. Aleesha's expression changes from being concerned to deflation, and as her posture drops, she lets go of Rachel's hand. Rachel's hand drops to the bed with a soft bounce, before slightly curling and staying at rest on the bed. Aleesha looks at Rachel's face and she stands.

Tears start to stream down her face. She brings her hands to touch the tears running down her face. She moves to her reflection in the window to see what she looks like. As she touches her face where tears are rolling down, she sees Rachel's reflection in the window. She turns around and then goes to hold Rachel's hand again.

Aleesha walks into Queens Park, dazed. She sits on a park bench, punches it, then cries while rubbing her fist. She wipes her eyes, and inspects the tear droplets as they drop on her hands. She's oblivious to anything happening around her and everything seems quiet or muted. She holds back waves of anxiety but lets through some waves of grief from time to time. As it gets dark, Aleesha tries to get comfortable. She rubs her arms to warm herself. She closes her eyes and falls asleep.

The next morning Aleesha watches families with young children play. She smiles at the laughter of young children and then gets teary as parents pick them up and cuddle and tickle them. Ruby who is an older woman who is homeless wanders past and Aleesha gives her a smile before Ruby feeds an increasing gathering of sulfur–crested cockatoos.

Later that afternoon, Aleesha scrolls on her phone. She stops at Quade's number. She looks around and then slides her finger on the phone to make the list move on, before throwing her phone away.

Aleesha goes and gets her phone and scrolls through some videos. She chooses a video about the life of a female octopus and presses play. The narrator starts, 'She's in her nursery den, with her hundred thousand eggs. She'll watch them, clean them, make sure they get all the oxygen that they need. She'll flick away anyone little, and put her life on the line against anyone big. Now. She's done it. She's made it. She got them there. They're hatching, and starting to leave. She'll never leave though. She's dying. She's been starving herself to look after them. This has been the last thing she's done on the curtain fall of her life. She has sacrificed herself, to give them... the best possible chance in life.'

Aleesha rubs her temples in pain, swipes out of the video and scrolls for Matthew's number. She pauses at his contact, then puts the phone down beside her. Aleesha picks the phone up, and goes to press the button to call him, but then stops and puts the phone down again. Aleesha picks the phone up, and sees that the battery is running low. She quickly presses the call button.

'It's Aleesha. Can you put me through to Matthew please?... Can you tell him to call Aleesha?'

Aleesha ends the call and lies back.

Aleesha's phone rings.

"Matthew.... I need somewhere to stay in town tonight.... No. I don't want you to send me a list of shelters to call. For fucks sake. They're fucking dangerous places, and I told you I'd never go to another one after.... Fucking hell Matthew. It's the f word. How the fuck do you expect to work with teenagers, and not expect to hear the f word.... Is your mother alive Matthew?... Great, because... because... because mine fucking isn't, and now I'm completely and utterly fucked, you stupid, fucking fuck fuck.... Ah fine. Have it your way. Go fuck yourself.

Aleesha drops the phone and punches the ground.

Aleesha walks into the church at night time and approaches Charlotte who turns to her. 'Hey!' Charlotte says. Charlotte gives Aleesha an excited hug that Aleesha doesn't love, but doesn't fight. 'I didn't think I was going to see you again!'

'Sorry bout that.'

Charlotte gets a bigger smile and gives her another hug.

'Don't be silly!'

Aleesha and Charlotte carry jugs of water to the tables.

'Remember when you asked how come I hung out with that lot?' Aleesha asks.

'And you said I had bad juju!'

'Yeah. Sorry about that.'

'There's nothing wrong with my juju!'

'I know that! Why else would I be talking to you? But I've been thinking about that heaps.'

'I bet.'

'You guys seemed different and more impressive than what I was used to, and I wanted to be... a part of something, I don't know, impressive... so that I could build a new life for myself, with people who can cope with me, if you know what I mean?'

'Sorry!'

'If anyone needs to feel sorry, it ain't you!'

'Yeah. You're right! They were making me look bad by association, the buggers! Sorry I didn't step in.... Um, how's your mum?'

'Even more like concrete... and I'm not at Quade's anymore.'

Charlotte looks shocked.

'When?'

'It seems that pushing people too hard, may not be working out for me. Apparently I should be doing something differently. Hmmm. Oh. When. Um.... Couple of days ago.'

'Why didn't you tell me already?'

'Fuck. I don't know. Not everything's about you Charlotte.'

Aleesha looks around agitatedly.

'You do know I like you, don't you?'

Aleesha looks down in front of her.

'Uhhh....'

'Who's looking after you?'

'Looking after me? Get real. I make people fuck up or fuck off, not look after me. People can't handle me it seems. I'm trying to be less scary, but it's not fuckin working. Can't seem to find the dial to turn down.'

'I meant, where are you staying?'

'Oh. Park.'

'Yeah. That's not right. You're coming back with us tonight.'

Aleesha sees Ben in the entrance. Their eyes meet, he turns on his heels, walking out quickly, and she runs after him.

Aleesha catches up to Ben.

'Ben!'

Ben stops and turns to face her.

'Is this where we're at?'

'Hey?'

'We don't talk anymore. Is that it?'

'Uh.... I'm not sure we have anything in... in....'

'Is it because I'm not your mum?'

'What?!'

'You want someone to nurse feed you like your mumma?'

'What the hell is wrong with you? You're so twisted.'

'Yeah, I'll take that. But at least I know how to adult. You've never had to, have you?'

'Hold on. What's so great about you again?'

Aleesha shakes her head quickly and shuts her eyes.

'Yeah.... I don't know.'

Ben looks up the street, and moves to leave. He turns back to Aleesha, then looks up the street again. Ben looks at Aleesha again. Aleesha turns and goes back inside.

CHAPTER XV

Rising

Conditions for growth

Aleesha is lying on her back on a bed in a spare room in Charlotte's family's home. Charlotte appears in the doorway.

'You don't have to stay in here.'

Aleesha doesn't hear.

'Aleesha.'

No response.

'Aleesha!'

Aleesha raises her head quickly.

'What?!'

'I've been here for five minutes.'

'Sorry. Dull roar in here.' Aleesha points to her head.

'Come out. You don't need to hide yourself away.'

Aleesha sits on the couch next to Charlotte. Aleesha turns to her.

'I need my own place, or I'm going to fuck up things with you too.'

'What? Don't be silly.'

'I'm not being silly. When I'm uncomfortable, everyone around me is. Then they resent me for it. Like it's my fault or something.'

'What do you want to do?'

'Live on my own.'

'Okay.'

'That way I can keep everything nice and simple.'

'You're really don't need to....'

'Charlotte. I know myself better than you do. If I say I'm gonna fuck up. I'm gonna.'

'Okay.'

'But getting my own place would be like pulling a sword from a rock because I'm so... bad, and stuff. Maybe I can sway Matthew's Team Leader Sue, the shot caller.'

Aleesha gets out her phone and rings it.

'Can I speak to Sue Kelly please? It's Aleesha.... Okay I'll wait.... Great. Thanks.'

'So?' Charlotte asks.

'She's in a meeting apparently, but said to call back at 4.'

Aleesha and Charlotte are sitting on the couch later in the afternoon.

'Oh shit. What's the time?'

Aleesha pulls out her phone. The time on the phone changes to 4:00pm. Aleesha dials a number.

'Sue?... I really could use some help.... I know I'm a teenager, but, my mum just died and I've got nowhere. Teenagers are people too.... Sue, for fu... sorry, Sue, did you want me to get onto my journo friend?... Okay, I'll meet with him but he better have something from you.'

Aleesha ends the call.

Matthew is sitting on a couch with a pen and paper opposite Aleesha and Charlotte.

'Um. What are your plans?'

'I need somewhere around here.'

'Why?'

'Why do you fu.... Sorry. Sorry. Sorry. Uhhh, because this is where I grew up, where my mum lived, and where this doofus is.'

Charlotte smiles. Matthew looks at Charlotte.

Aleesha continues, 'I found something online about supported accommodation? I'm 16 now, so how do we get that happening?'

'Good work! Sue gave me the names for a few of those places.'

'Wow...! And they don't have a habit of kicking people out, do they?'

'They have rules like everyone, but less than you've had, because they only take you if they think that you can keep it together by yourself with only small bits of help.'

'The less I have someone breathing down my neck waiting for to me to fuck up by losing my shit with them, the better. Anyhoo. What else do you need from me?'

'Education. Sue said you really to need to be involved in some education, for us to set you up.'

'I've been looking at college courses in childcare.'

'You have?' Charlotte asks.

'I figured I could use my scariness to keep little people safe, instead of just fucking up my own life. Just like you Matthew. Well not entirely like you, because you never learnt scary. I meant keeping people safe.'

'Thanks. Ummm. I'll get your profile to the supported accommodation providers, and organize for you to attend an info session on studying childcare.'

'Ummm... that profile. How bad is it these days?'

Matthew laughs and then pulls it in.

'Well. It hasn't improved, has it?!'

'Can we just shorten it up? I don't want to mess up my chances of getting in.'

'We have to tell them about all your behaviours, to cover ourselves. You know that.'

Matthew pulls out a different piece of paper.

'Okay, what do we have here.... Absconding, verbal and physical aggression, kicking, punching, and head-butting, property damage, self-harm, mental health, criminal activity, self-placing.'

Charlotte is looking at Aleesha. Aleesha and Charlotte are sitting in silence, then Aleesha throws her head back at the couch and puts her hands on her head.

'Shit!... There's no way I'm going to get anywhere.'

'Well let's see hey?'

Matthew leaves the room.

'I'm so screwed,' Aleesha says to Charlotte.

CHAPTER XVI

Collaboration

Greater than the sum

Aleesha and Charlotte are setting up tables and chairs for the soup kitchen at church. Aleesha keeps returning to her phone on one of the tables, to check if there are any missed calls. Aleesha's phone rings and she runs to it.

'…. Wait. All three of them?…. You're serious?… Shit!'

Aleesha hangs up and turns to Charlotte.

'One of them has a vacancy, but they're concerned about my behaviours…. So they've said "no".'

Aleesha heads towards the front door with tears in her eyes.

Aleesha sits on the side of the street, She looks up to see Ruby who reaches down and squeezes her shoulder. Aleesha smiles and places her hand on Ruby's. Ruby heads inside. Charlotte comes to Aleesha.

'There must be a way,' Aleesha says.

Charlotte shrugs.

'I've been making good choices more. Well... I've been doing more adulting if nothing else!... Maybe.... Um.... How about I do a reference from you and your dad, fine upstanding citizens that you are, to tell them about my social work skills and stuff? Would that be okay?'

'Mmmmm....'

'Charlotte! You've been getting free labour out me. It's the leas....'

'I'm stirring you, dopey! Of course that's fine. My dad's very impressed with you.'

'He is?!'

Charlotte smiles and nods.

'You may have even taken out top spot from me,'

'Shut up! No I haven't!'

Charlotte laughs. Aleesha rings Matthew.

'Charlotte and her dad are going to write references for me, to talk about how much of a model fucking citizen I am these days!... Great. We'll get them through soon.' Aleesha ends the call.

'He said that might help. Thanks Charlotte!'

Aleesha starts to write an email.

Aleesha watches people walking past while she twirls her hair at the front of church. She answers her phone.

'You gottem okay?... Great.... Awww, hell no. Do they have to?... But I don't live there anymore.... I know, I know. But they're just gonna tell them where I fucked up. Nothing good…. Yeah. Yep. Fuck. But Matthew, you gotta talk them out of it. Seriously.'

Aleesha kicks the kerb and hangs up.

The church has filled up and Charlotte and Aleesha are serving. Aleesha's phone glows. She runs to a quieter part of the church hall.

'Who's this?… Wow. Thanks for calling me!…. Yeah…. Yep…. Yeah. I'm here now. It's a big turn out tonight!… Okay…. Really?… You sure?… Really? I mean, awesome. Sure. Thanks!'

Aleesha runs back to Charlotte and picks her up and gives her a tight hug, before breaking into tears.

'They're considering a trial.'

'No way!'

'Way!'

The next day at Charlotte's house, Aleesha draws a bull in a china shop. Charlotte brings her a bowl of chips and sits beside her.

'Has Matthew called yet?'

'If he makes me wait one more day, I'm going down there and breaking into his building and dragging him out! Doesn't he care about my fucking nerves?'

'Easy there.'

'Sorry. Sorry!'

Aleesha's phone rings and she grabs it.

'Fuck! It's just Kim.'

Aleesha answers.

'What?!... Nah, you're right. Just waiting on fucking Matthew. He's taking ages.... I'll call later.'

Aleesha hangs up.

Aleesha has almost finished her drawing. Her phone rings. She looks at Charlotte who folds her hands, and Aleesha answers.

'Matthew?!... Really?!... You're not shitting me are you?!'

It's the next day when Matthew opens the door to a unit while Aleesha and Charlotte holding Aleesha's belongings in bags, peer around to check out the surroundings before following him in. Aleesha and Charlotte investigate inside and return to Matthew who hands Aleesha a set of keys.

'Welcome to the real world!'

'That sounds like a good place to be if I've been somewhere else till now. Thanks!'

Aleesha sits on the floor with Charlotte.

'You've got my mobile. Call me if you need anything.... Aleesha?'

'Yeah?'

'You were serious about starting studying childcare next Tuesday, weren't you?'

'Yeah, of course!'

Aleesha nods to assure Matthew. He breaks eye contact.

'Awesome....'

Matthew is lost in thought and looks sad.

'Matthew? You right?'

'Uh. Yeah. It's. It's just that you, you've always had the most potential out of any of the kids that I work with. And. And I don't want you to screw that up. Okay?'

Aleesha is shocked and a tear comes to her eye.

'You've got this Leesh. You're gonna make it!'

Aleesha averts her eyes, still looking touched. Matthew smiles, opens the door and leaves as Kim walks in.

'Surprise!' Kim says.

Aleesha gets a big smile and stands.

'Kim! Did you finally go your own way? I told you you could!'

'Nah. Matthew brought me up and I've been waiting round the corner.'

'Matthew hey?'

Aleesha walks to the open door, and looks out to see if she can still see Matthew but he has disappeared.

'How long you before you go back?' Aleesha asks Kim.

'That depends on you!'

Aleesha's smile broadens.

'Wow. Charlotte. This is Kim. My previous fellow detainee! He's all grown up! Look at him!'

'I'm older than her....'

'I've heard a lot about you,' Charlotte offers.

Kim blushes at Charlotte then turns back to Aleesha.

'Uh. So.... What's it like having your own place?'

'I'll tell you when it sinks in. Trouble is. I'd rather be outside. Picnic Point anyone?!'

CHAPTER XVII

Loss

Past and future

Aleesha and Charlotte walk out to the viewing platform at Picnic Point and Aleesha takes Charlotte's hand with her skateboard in the other. Kim follows with his scooter.

'So romantical! I'm gonna miss rage you know? It's a really hard thing to quit. Even though most of her died already.'

'Who?' Kim asks.

Aleesha's eyes moisten.

'Her mum,' Charlotte says.

'Race you round that rose bed and back,' Kim offers.

Charlotte gives Kim a frustrated look, but neither he or Aleesha notice. Kim sets off. Aleesha takes a moment, then flies after him. She slides her board sideways to get around the bed quicker than him, but the board catches and flips throwing her hard into the ground. Kim stops and

Charlotte runs to Aleesha. Aleesha sits up and Charlotte places her hand on her shoulder.

'You right?'

'I don't think she figured out that I'm not that bad. A little fucked up maybe... but not completely nothing.'

Charlotte looks confused.

'Sophie.... She didn't get that I'm not... um... useless.'

'I wonder if she knows that I have my own place now.... She still lives with her parents... and she's older than me.'

Kim approaches.

'You lose!' Kim says triumphantly.

'Shut up Kim,' Charlotte says.

Aleesha looks at Charlotte in surprise then turns to Kim.

'Shut up Kim!'

Aleesha laughs and meets eyes with Charlotte who laughs as well.

'At least you're the same Leesh.'

'I screwed up with mum t....' Aleesha starts.

Aleesha stares blankly.

'Are you going to, like, stop, like, being able to cope with me too?' Aleesha asks Charlotte.

'It's awkward you asked, because, um... I can't promise anything.'

Aleesha looks at Charlotte sadly and then they both burst out laughing.

'And fuck you too! I don't deserve it but I'm really hoping that you can keep tolerating me, and not wilt. Even my mum was better than me at getting people to like her and stick around. Why I'm having such trouble, I don't know. I mean, yeah yeah, be less scary Aleesha. You're so big and powerful.'

'You're okay.'

'The scary thing....'

'Yeah?'

'Is that, I may, have actually enjoyed emptying the shit out of my head. It just felt like a truck, dumping, and dumping, and dumping, and covering her up, so... so that I don't have to see her anymore.'

Aleesha gets teary, and tries to shake out of it. She looks nervously at Charlotte.

'But I can't do that anymore. I can't keep pushing people past their breaking point.... That really fucks up my life.'

Aleesha's tears increase. Charlotte looks pained.

'I kicked her.'

'What?! Who?'

'Sophie. After she was raining down on you at the park.'

'Wow. Kim!'

Aleesha turns back to Charlotte.

'You're a Christian!'

'You gotta do what you gotta do sometimes. I guess?'

'You're asking the wrong person. You know I'm not doing great in that area. Don't do that again but. Okay? You're better. Try to make good choices?!'

CHAPTER XVIII

Coming together

Like minds

Aleesha and Charlotte sit on a park bench at Picnic Point.

'Anyone hungry?' Charlotte asks

'I've got it! Finally!' Aleesha says.

'Uh oh.'

'No, really! My brain has been chewing on this in the background for ages. Charlotte, you remember Sophie thinking that Ruby was rude for not letting her touch her stuff?'

Charlotte nods.

'Ruby is cool, and I reckon she'd do me the favour.... Oooh. Even better. Brain poppin goin on in here. Everyone queue the fuck up!'

'Um....'

'So. Can you get your dad to call Sophie's mum for us to take it next level? I've been racking my brains for ages now, trying to figure out how to get her where....'

Charlotte looks suspicious.

'Remember you're still on a trial,' Charlotte admonishes.

The following week an elderly man approaches the church door which has a sign. 'Soup Kitchen tonight will be held at 26 Jellicoe Street, North Toowoomba. 5pm.'

Aleesha rides her board down the middle of Ruthven Street with Charlotte and Kim flanking. Charlotte is on a BMX bike and Kim is on his scooter.

Sophie is reading a book in her lounge room and hears the doorbell. She goes to the door.

Ruby is standing at the front door, holding her bags as Sophie opens it.

'What are you doing here?' Sophie asks.

Ruby doesn't answer and tries to push past, but Sophie keeps blocking her.

Her mother Ruth comes to the door just having returned from work 'Sophie! Let her in!'

Ruby successfully pushes past Sophie.

'Sorry I forgot to tell you that I agreed with Lou to host the soup kitchen here tonight.'

Sophie takes a moment to process.

'Mum?'

'Yes dear.'

'But why, you know, here?'

'But they're so, I don't know. Dirty?'

Ruth freezes. She looks at Ruby. She goes to mumble an apology but runs out of ideas so she shakes her head and disappears to get changed.

Ruby decides the debate is over, so heads for the back. Sophie watches on in horror. Ruby puts her bags down inside the pool gate and swishes her feet in the pool.

Sophie hears the door bell, opens the door and in files group after group who have arrived for the meal, filling the lounge room and some heading for the kitchen and pool. Sophie hears the door bell and heads for the door. Sophie opens the door, exasperated. She is shocked to see Aleesha with Kim and Charlotte. Aleesha brings out a bunch of flowers from behind her back.

'A peace offering.... I hope no one's touched your stuff?!'

Sophie looks confused and then from Aleesha to Charlotte.

'She's really sorry about the whole kicking you thing,' Aleesha contributes.

'Sorry Sophie. That was bad of me,' Charlotte offers.

Sophie looks carefully back at Aleesha with a few checks back on Charlotte.

'I've been trying to teach her that aggression isn't the answer,' Aleesha explains with a sweet smile.

118

'Sophie....' Ruth calls out.

Sophie looks over her shoulder, takes the flowers, and stands aside for them to enter.

Aleesha tenses as she passes Sophie and starts to slow a little. Charlotte notices so she quickly pokes Aleesha in the kidneys to keep going. Aleesha smiles back over her shoulder at Charlotte.

'What?!'

Aleesha keeps her pace up and they continue in.

Lou and the rest of the staff from the soup kitchen carry in prepared food behind them.

Aleesha, Charlotte, and Kim mingle with the guests. Sophie starts to warm and increasingly interact with the guests, while still looking nervous and keeping some distance from Aleesha.

Aleesha and Charlotte head for the pool. Aleesha sits down besides Ruby on the edge of the pool. Charlotte and Kim sit besides Aleesha. Aleesha smiles at Ruby and Ruby returns to swishing her legs in the water.

THE END